I0670605

Persuasions

VARIOUS INTENTIONS

AE LISTER

Various Intentions
ISBN # 978-1-80250-982-3
©Copyright AE Lister 2022
Cover Art by Kelly Martin ©Copyright September 2022
Interior text design by Claire Siemaszkiewicz
Pride Publishing

VARIOUS
INTENTIONS

Dedication

To Friendship.

Chapter One

Staking out your pseudo-child on their last day of exams for their final year in high school was a parental right-of-passage. And if it wasn't, it should have been.

"Has he texted you?" I asked Vincent, as we waited in the car for Taylor to emerge from the red brick building.

"Not yet," Vincent said, leaning forward to keep an eye out. "He was planning to catch the bus home, so I want to make sure we don't miss him."

"There he is," Matteo said with composure from the back seat.

Taylor had burst forth from the double doors of the alternative secondary school and bent down to tie his shoe, his puffy blue jacket unzipped.

"I can't believe he wears runners in winter," I said. "He's going to fall and break his little neck."

I reached past Vincent and slammed the middle of the steering wheel, causing the horn to blast and Taylor to spasm and glare at the source of the alarming sound.

Vincent had lowered the window and now leaned his head out. "That was Nic. Blame him."

Taylor made a gesture of resignation as he stood and ambled to the car. "What are you doing here?"

"Why aren't you wearing boots?" I asked. He ignored me.

Matteo leaned forward from the back seat. "It's your last high school exam, Taylor. We're taking you out for supper."

I leaned over Vincent, ignoring his long-suffering expression. "We have reservations at Moxies. Not super fancy, I know, but the servers are hot and I know you—"

"Yes! I love Moxies!" Taylor pumped the air and opened the back door of the car, passing his backpack to Matteo then sliding in beside my other romantic partner. "Hi, Dad. I mean, Dads."

"*I'm* not your dad," Vincent said, starting the engine and pulling into the road. Vincent was Taylor's cousin and my live-in boyfriend. Matteo had insinuated himself into the relationship just after Taylor had joined the household to escape his uber-religious parents.

"You act like my dad. And it's just easier to call all three of you 'Dad'."

"Fine." Vincent shrugged. "Whatever."

"But who's your Daddy, Taylor?" I said, waggling my brows. Taylor and I had a weird relationship.

"Ew, gross."

I smirked at him. "You used to be intrigued by me and what I got up to with the other dads in private. What happened?"

He made a face. "I got a glimpse of the reality. God, I almost threw up in my mouth just now, thinking about it."

8

"Careful," I said.

"Why? You gonna punish me?"

"I'm sure I can think of something not sex-related to make you watch your tongue, brat."

"Matteo, Nic is being mean to me," Taylor said, opening a bottle of water he'd pulled from his bag and tipping it to his lips.

"Don't bring me into this," Matteo sighed.

"You're in this car, aren't you?"

"Yes, and I'm starting to wish I wasn't."

"Nice. That's really nice. Don't you want to wish me a happy graduation?" Taylor said, snuggling into Matteo, who put an arm around him and kissed the top of his head.

"Of course. Happy graduation, Taylor."

"That's assuming you passed the exam," I pointed out.

Taylor narrowed his eyes at me in the rearview mirror. "I passed. You think I want to spend another minute in high school? I'm already finishing six months late."

Vincent glanced at his younger cousin in the back seat. "You've worked hard, and you should be proud of yourself."

Taylor blushed and smiled shyly. "Oh, pish. You know, I don't want to live with you all forever."

I put a hand to my heart. "Taylor, you wound me."

"No offense, but I'd like to move out on my own at some point. Not yet, though."

"Of course. But you'd better plan to come for dinner with your dads once a week, at least," I muttered. I'd been the last person to think I'd want a teenager in the house, and now I couldn't imagine our lives without Taylor.

Taylor cuddled up next to Matteo and kissed his cheek. "For Matteo's cooking? You bet. Even if Vincent cooks. But if Nic cooks…"

"Watch yourself, little one." I laughed, because he was right about my failed attempts at putting together appealing meals, on the rare occasions I'd tried. Most days Matteo cooked dinner, and if he couldn't, Vincent or Taylor did. I was last on the list for a reason.

Matteo had come to us when Vincent had injured his hand, and Daphne had suggested someone to help with the cooking and domestic duties. We'd then invited Matteo into our bedroom and things had progressed from there. Now the three of us were in a committed poly relationship with Taylor to look after, and I'd never been happier.

"Oh please, you've been threatening to give me a spanking since I moved in. But I think you're worried you'd like it too much."

"Taylor," Vincent warned.

"There are many different ways I can make your life miserable, Taylor. Don't tempt me."

Verbally sparring with Taylor had become a daily diversion, and I'd miss it when he finally did move out.

Moxie's had a booth waiting for us. We took off our winter jackets and hung them on the nearby hook. Just before Vincent slid onto the bench, I nudged him in the ribs. "Hey, remember what we did in the bathroom the last time we were here?"

As I'd expected, a blush rose in his cheeks, and he glanced at the others to see if they'd heard. Matteo avoided his gaze while fighting a smile, and, to my amusement, Taylor looked shocked.

He leaned over the table, his eyebrows raised. "A *public* bathroom?"

I shrugged. "We were alone for most of it."

"*Most* of it?" Taylor sputtered and sat down, shaking his head. "God, you guys are turning me into a prude. *I'm* the one who's supposed to be fucking people in bathrooms. I'm eighteen and horny and —"

"I didn't fuck Vincent in the bathroom," I said calmly.

"Oh. Okay," Taylor said. "Good."

He pretended to focus on the menu, but he kept glancing up at us, and I knew it was killing him to pretend he wasn't curious as hell.

"Can we order, please?" Vincent said, with some embarrassment.

I scanned the menu. "Of course. I'm going to order extra aioli with whatever I'm getting — because there's two of you, now." I winked at Matteo.

Taylor stood up. "I'm going to the bathroom." He pointed a finger at me. "*You* stay where you are."

Matteo and Vincent glared at me while Taylor headed for the men's room.

"What?"

"This is supposed to be a celebration of Taylor finishing his high school credits," Matteo said gently. "Not a confessional for all the kinky things you've done to Vincent."

I shrugged. "I mean, *all* the kinky —"

Matteo pushed his knife forward slightly. "But please do share the details with me later."

"Oh, God," Vincent moaned, covering his face.

I finger-gunned Matteo. "You got it."

When Taylor came back, I apologized and offered to have his guitar restrung as penance.

"Don't be dumb. It's fine." Taylor nodded at Vincent. "It's kind of worth my own cringe to see

Vincent so embarrassed, when I *know* the kinky bastard was fully on board with whatever happened."

"Oh, and, Taylor?"

"Yeah?"

I pointed out of the window. "See that silver Honda?"

Taylor focused on the car that sparkled in the late evening sunshine. "Yeah?"

"That's your *real* graduation present."

"Oh, that's hilarious," Taylor said, turning back as Matteo placed a Honda fob on a rainbow key ring onto the table in front of him.

He looked at it and scooped it up in his fingers. "What the fuck is this? Is this some kind of a joke? I'm going to kill you guys."

"It's not a joke," Vincent said.

"The car's yours," I confirmed, sitting up straighter. "It's a couple of years old, but there's barely any mileage on it. Vincent had it detailed so it's shiny and clean, inside and out, although it won't stay that way with all the winter slush on the roads."

Taylor stared at the fob in his hand. Then he looked at the car through the window. Then he looked at me with shining eyes and a tremulous lip.

"Really?" he whispered, as if he couldn't quite believe it.

Matteo put an arm around him and kissed him on the cheek. "You deserve it. You've worked hard and you've helped out at the house, too. You're almost as good a cook as me, now."

Taylor stared at the Honda device for another few seconds. "Oh my God. What! A car? *A car!*" He slid out of the booth and started leafing through the coats for his jacket. "I want to see it!"

"I'll take you," Vincent said. "Nic, can you please order for me? You know what I like." He took his jacket from the hook and passed Taylor his.

"I certainly do. What do you want to eat, Taylor?"

"I don't care. Order me anything," he said, shoving his arms in the sleeves of his blue puffer jacket and racing out of the restaurant with Vincent on his trail.

"That was a success," Matteo said, smiling and pretending to look over the menu, although we ate here so often that I was sure he already knew what he was going to order. "It was a good idea, Nic."

"Honestly, having only my car between the four of us was becoming a problem, even though you don't drive. Now that Taylor has his own, we don't have to worry about not having a means of transportation while he's out galivanting."

We watched Taylor circle the car while Vincent pointed out certain things, then he opened the driver's door and slid inside. Vincent leaned on the door, laughing and grinning. He glanced into the restaurant and gave us a thumbs-up.

"He's worked so hard, and now he's graduated high school. He's got a job lined up and a plan to attend college in the fall. He's a good kid, Matteo." I put my chin in my hand. "I never thought I wanted to be a dad, but it seems to come naturally with Taylor."

Matteo grinned. "It's nice that we can split the responsibility three ways."

"It is. Absolutely. I'm starting to think poly relationships should be the standard, especially in this economy."

When Vincent brought Taylor back inside, the kid slid onto my lap and gave me the tightest hug, regardless of the audience. "Thank you so much, Nic. I love it. It's perfect."

He was rosy and cold from being outside. I hugged him back, then nudged him off.

"I'm glad you like it. You deserve it. But we have to sit down and go over some rules when we get home."

"Sure. Okay."

"And you need to give your other daddy a hug, because the car is from all of us."

Taylor hung up his jacket again, slid into the booth beside Matteo and wrapped him in his arms. "Thank you, Favorite Dad. You are the best."

Matteo chuckled, and I pretended not to hear the endearment. Matteo *was* probably Taylor's favorite. He was just so 'Dad-like'—forthright and steady—whereas Vincent and I were more scattered and impulsive.

Taylor worked hard to contain himself through the meal, because he was dying to drive his 'new' car. So we didn't order dessert, and Vincent went with Taylor in the new car while I drove Matteo back to our place.

We beat them home and waited outside the front door for Taylor to pull in. When he got out of the driver's side, he was beaming.

"So? How does it drive?" I asked.

"Like a fucking dream," Taylor replied. "Thank you, guys, *so* much. It's amazing."

I wagged my finger at him. "No driving drunk or high. And you still have to be home by midnight if you're not sleeping at Riley's."

"Fine."

"And no texting while driving."

"Duh."

We went inside, and Matteo put on a pot of tea while Taylor phoned his boyfriend.

"Hello, babe," Riley answered, on speaker.

"I got a fucking *car* for graduation!" Taylor yelled into the phone.

"What? No way!" Riley replied. "You lucky ass."

Taylor laughed.

"*New* car?" Riley said.

"Nah, second-hand. But almost new. A Honda Civic. Silver. Wait, I'll show you." Taylor got up and headed out of the door.

"Put on a jacket!" I said, as the door slammed behind him. I rolled my eyes. "Well, the car was a hit," I said, leaning back on the sofa.

"Were you worried?" Vincent said with a smile.

"Not really. Cars *are* generally an impressive gift."

My phone vibrated, and I fished it out of my pocket, knowing who it was by the tones of *Sympathy for the Devil* that invaded the silence.

"Hey, Daf. What's up?" I said, bringing it to my ear.

"Did you give Sparky his car? What did he say? Was he surprised?"

"He was surprised. Didn't expect it at all. He repeated himself a lot. It was cute."

"Nice! I'm so glad he's happy. He's worked hard."

"Yes, he has."

"Look... I need you to meet me for coffee. Soon!"

I recognized a certain something in the tone of Daphne's voice—the same something that had been there when she'd called to persuade me to meet this 'cute as shit' client of hers who'd turned out to be Vincent. "Why?"

"I can't explain it over the phone."

"Well, Jesus. That's a first." I snorted.

"Very funny. Can you meet me tomorrow?"

"Well, I have to work…"

"You get a lunch, don't you?"

"But I have marking to do."

"Oh, come on. I'll buy you lunch."

"Well, in that case."

"I'll come to your office. See you around noon."

"Sure. See you. Bye." There was no point arguing. I'd end up agreeing anyway.

Matteo brought in the tea and placed it on the coffee table.

"What did Daphne want?"

I stared at the phone, wondering that myself.

"Well, I'm not sure. Wanted to know how Taylor reacted to his gift. But she's making me meet her for lunch tomorrow for some reason."

Daphne was my longtime friend who worked as a professional Domme, had introduced me to Vincent and reamed out my ex-boyfriend after he'd started dicking me around. I loved her so much and would do anything for her, such as letting her set up a sex dungeon in my basement for almost a month the previous year.

Daphne had a flair for the dramatic and intense, even outside of her lucrative business.

Matteo, who had been a member of our rather unconventional relationship for a good eight months now, had gotten a promotion at his job. He was now a senior-level market researcher for a well-known software company. That kept him busy during the regular work week, but his evenings and weekends remained free so that he could come home, cook dinner for us and help with domestic chores.

Vincent, who had been a full-time domestic service person for me since we'd moved in together, received a regular wage on top of his room and board, as well as enjoyable bonuses from Matteo and me, so that we made quite the spectacular and functional family unit.

Taylor, who added to the overall atmosphere with his dry wit and explicit humor, had thrived under our admittedly neglectful care. He was a young adult now and disappeared most evenings into his room or went out with his boyfriend and other peers. But when he did grace us with his presence, he was respectful and cheerful, and I wondered how we had lived without him. We knew it was only a matter of time before he moved out on his own, or in with Riley, but now that he had his own car to take back and forth, he seemed content to keep things as they were, which made me happy in an unexpected way.

I'd never wanted children, but falling into a vague parenting schema with Taylor had been so natural and organic that it didn't seem strange at all and fulfilled me in some obscure way. I tried not to second-guess it.

* * * *

Daphne showed up early for our lunch date, peeking into my office like a student with a bad average.

"I see you there," I said without looking up from the paper I was grading.

"Oh, hey, Nic. You look very professional."

"I should hope so. This is my job." I put the pen down and looked at her.

Daphne stood in the doorway to my office. She was dressed in an elegant gray wool wrap coat and heeled leather boots that reached her knees. Her chestnut hair was pulled back in a high ponytail and a pair of sunglasses was perched atop her head.

"You can come in and have a seat, you know."

"Yeah, that's okay. I'm having flashbacks to high school." She thumbed over her shoulder. "Let's go eat."

"All right. Fine. I have to be back to teach a class at two."

"I will have you back long before that," she assured me, hooking her hand in my arm when I passed by.

"You look lovely, by the way," I said.

"Why, thank you, professor. You look edible, also."

I smiled at the predictable nature of our exchange.

We walked to a nearby café that made sandwiches as well as fancy original drinks. We paid for a couple of paninis and two coffees. Once we'd found a table and taken off our coats, I sat back and regarded Daphne with a quizzical expression.

"So, what's too important to talk about over the phone?" I was truly curious. This was unprecedented. Normally, she told me all sorts of things over the phone.

To my utter amazement, Daphne blushed and squirmed in her seat.

"Oh my God."

"What?" she said, frowning and shifting again. She glanced behind her to see what had so amazed me.

"Who the hell are you and what have you done with Daphne?"

She realized I was messing with her and gave me a look. "Oh, that's funny."

"You're blushing."

"I am not. It's cold out."

"We're inside."

"Nic...stop. I need you to be serious."

I leaned forward, curious as all hell as to what Daphne wanted to talk about.

"I'm very serious. What is so important you needed to get me into a booth at a restaurant to tell me?"

Daphne opened her mouth, sighed, then closed it. She adjusted her seat again. Irritation began to bubble inside me.

"Daf, sit still and tell me what is wrong."

She continued to hem and haw until I slapped my hand on the table, making her jump and eliciting dirty looks from other patrons.

"You probably don't know that I've often fantasized about hauling you over my knee, pulling down your panties and walloping that pert backside."

She parted her rouged lips and inhaled a gasp. "Nic! Really?"

I grinned. "Maybe. Sure. And I'll do it if you don't tell me what you dragged me here to tell me."

Her eyes narrowed. "I'm not scared of you."

I shrugged and drilled her with a Dom glare. She didn't hold out very long.

"Fine. I'll tell you. It's...it's embarrassing." She looked everywhere but at me.

"Tell me."

She nodded, licked her lips. "I think I'm in love."

That was the *last* thing I had expected Daphne to say.

"You're — you're *what*?"

She threw me a smile like a debutante at her first cotillion...and *giggled*.

"I'm in love. I think. Probably. Maybe?" She dropped her chin in her hand and giggled again.

I was speechless. I stared at her for a long moment.

Daphne didn't *do* love. Daphne did torture and domination and impact play and orgasm control—but she didn't do *love*.

"What? How? *Who?*" I stuttered. Who could possibly have stolen the heart of the city's most enigmatic Dominatrix?

Daphne sighed. "One of my clients." She made a comical face of distress.

"Oh wow. God. That's...awkward?"

"I know!" she wailed. "I don't know what the fuck to do! Or how it happened. Or why. Or how. Oh, God, Nic! Help."

She seemed so adrift and confused that I reached a hand across the table and enfolded her narrow, talented fingers in my palm.

"Hey, it's okay. I mean, worse things have happened, right?"

She didn't seem convinced. "Maybe?"

"Is the guy even—wait a second. *Is* it a guy?"

"It's a guy...in every sense of the word."

I put a hand to my chest. "That hurts, Daphne."

"Oh, no, I didn't mean in *that* way! You know I don't define gender like that. I just mean— God, I don't even know what I mean. That's how confused I am, Nic."

"Is he even available? Aren't a lot of the men who come to you in committed, supposedly monogamous, relationships?" I used air quotes to indicate just how committed those relationships were.

"Yes, but he's single, as far as I know. I don't think he's interested in anything more than some fun and a few orgasms. *That's* the problem. How do I let him know that I want more? He may see it as a betrayal of our business arrangement."

"Hmm-m."

"Hmm-m, what? Hmm-m, you're just as confused as I am, or hmm-m, you've thought of a solution?"

"It might not be a solution, but it would let you know where he stood on things."

"What? Tell me!" She clasped my hand in both of hers, her gaze imploring and desperate.

I laughed.

"I'm glad you find this so amusing," she said.

"I'm sorry. But why don't you tell him you can't be his Dominatrix anymore because you've developed feelings for him? See what he says to that."

Daphne stared at me for a long moment. "Fuck."

"What?"

"Why didn't I think of that?"

I laughed again and raised my eyebrows. "Because you are absolutely twitterpated, and it's fucking adorable."

"Twitter-*what*-ed?" She made a face.

"It's from *Bambi*. I think."

She arched an eyebrow. "Really. I'm *not* a fucking Disney princess."

I smiled knowingly. "I think that maybe you *are*."

Daphne sighed and sat back in her seat. She seemed more in control of herself.

"So, are you going to tell me this gentleman's name? And what's so special about him?"

"He's—older."

"Do tell."

"He's, like, in his fifties."

"Really?"

"Yes. Oh, Nic, he's so wonderful. He's handsome and funny and understands who he is, you know?"

"That can be the benefit of being older, I suppose." I took a drink. "Although, you seem to have figured yourself out fairly early on."

She gave me a wicked grin. "I started exploring at a very young age."

"You little minx."

She leaned across the table and grabbed me by the lapels of my jacket. "Nic, what am I gonna do?"

"I don't know. But that suggestion I gave you is sound."

"But...but what if he leaves and I never see him again?"

"Well, then, you won't be compromising your business principles by falling in love with your client. Look... You might as well find out whether he has any of the same feelings you do."

I quickly checked over my shoulder to make sure nobody was listening to us before I continued.

"I've got a problem of my own," I said, since I didn't get to talk one-on-one to Daphne often. At least, not in person.

That got her attention. She made a face.

"What problem can you possibly have, Nic? You have two lovely boyfriends and a young man who looks to you as a father and adores the hell out of you."

"What? He does? Really?" I was never sure what Taylor thought of me. Most of the time he acted like he barely tolerated me.

"Oh, Nic. Sparky thinks the world of you."

I grinned at Daphne's nickname for Taylor, who sometimes assisted in her sex dungeon wearing a leather pup hood and atrociously tight shorts, for the amusement of her clients.

"Well, that's good."

"So…what's up with you? Not enjoying Matteo's cooking anymore? Or is there a problem with his special sauce?"

I pretended to be shocked. "Daphne."

"Well?"

"It's not so specific. Is there…?" I thought about how to phrase my question. "Is there something like 'Dom burnout'? I mean, is it a thing?"

"Oh. Well, yeah. You can burn out doing anything." Her eyes widened. "Oh. Wow. Do you think you —?"

"I don't know. I'm finding it harder to get motivated with scenes. I feel like the three of us have already done everything — which can't possibly be true. But any time I think of something that pushes the envelope, I worry that it'll be too far and one of my beautiful men will mutiny…or both."

She gave me a sympathetic look.

"And, frankly, sometimes I'm just tired — like, actually tired. And I can't face doing a whole scene. But I don't want them to feel like I'm just dialing it in, either."

"Aw, Nic. You know, you're not going to be perfect."

I frowned, then sighed. "Sometimes that's hard for me to accept."

"I know it is," Daphne replied, sipping her coffee. "But you're a human person."

"A tired human person."

"And you're getting older…"

"Now hold on a second —"

"We *all* are."

I narrowed my eyes at Daphne. "I'm only thirty-five. You're almost forty."

Daphne's gaze turned glacial. "Yes, but I'm not experiencing Dom burnout."

I shrugged. "I don't even know if that's what's happening. Maybe I just need a vacation."

"Can you take one?"

"Not right now. The new term starts next week."

"Hmm." Daphne smiled and reached out a hand to rest on my forearm. "You could try relaxing the dynamic."

"Huh?"

"Like, loosen things up a bit. You don't always have to play by the rules."

I thought about that for a moment. "You mean, like, don't use all the regular protocols?"

"Exactly. Just be together in whatever way seems organic at the time."

It made sense. We'd done that on occasion, of course, but seemed to want to fall back into the protocols. Or maybe that was just me, feeling like we should.

"Maybe you're right."

"Let the two of them take over...or one of them. Switch things up. That would help."

I narrowed my eyes at her. "How do you, the mistress of protocols, know this?"

"I don't know. But a relationship is rather different from what I do."

"Rather."

She shrugged and sipped her specialty coffee. "I imagine that trying to keep to very specific roles in any long-term relationship is not going to work. You know what they say... '*Variety is the spice of life*'."

"Oh. Well, I thought that meant switching up toys and bondage positions."

"That won't hurt, either. But try other ways of switching things up."

"It's a good idea."

"I do have them."

Chapter Two

Taylor loved his car. He'd even named the damn thing. Every time he went out, he waggled his keys and announced he was taking 'Bailey' for a spin. It was kind of adorable, kind of geeky and kind of weird. But I was glad he appreciated his graduation gift.

"So is Bailey supposed to be a girl or a guy?" I asked one evening as we finished cleaning up from supper.

"Duh. Bailey's a skinny, sparkly twink that can't take no for an answer but loves me with all his heart."

"Wow," I said.

Vincent shook his head with resignation while Matteo chuckled.

"What?" Taylor said. "If straight guys can name cars and boats after girls, I can name my car after a sparkly twink, can't I?"

"If you want to be as basic as a straight guy."

Taylor snorted. "Huh. As if. I don't think I have to worry about that."

The doorbell rang and I muttered, "No, you probably don't," as I went to answer it.

Outside, in a puffy jacket similar to Taylor's but strawberry red, stood a slight young man who wouldn't have looked out of place on the cover of a men's magazine. He looked familiar in a vague way.

"Is Nic Walker here?" Stress emanated off the man, and he didn't attempt to smile, only gazed at me with imploring brown eyes. "I'm Juno's boyfriend, Charles."

That's when everything slotted into place. I'd met Charles at Juno's most recent gallery show, when I'd dressed Vincent like Tom Holland on *Lip Sync Battle*.

"Oh right! Come inside."

"Thank you. I'm really sorry to bother you." He didn't make any move to take his jacket off.

"Is everything all right?"

"I'm so sorry to bother you…"

"What's going on, Charles?"

He sighed. "Juno's locked me out, and you were the only person I could think of who might know how to talk to them? Calm them down, somehow?"

Charles' very pretty face was drawn and his features tight. If Juno had indeed done what Charles said, I could see why. "They do tend to be dramatic."

"They've never done this to me before. I don't know what the problem is. I haven't done anything that should make them mad—not on this level, anyway."

"Fuck. This is another one of Juno's mental health crises. They always start this way." I reached into the closet and grabbed my coat.

"You don't think they'd—?" Charles said, putting his fingers to his lips, his eyes going wide.

"I don't think so. But I want to talk to them and make sure they're okay."

Charles' features relaxed ever so slightly. "Thank you, Nic. Thank you!"

"Matteo, I have to go check on Juno. I don't know what's going on, but Charles is out of his depth at the moment."

Matteo came out of the kitchen, wiping his hands with a dish towel, and regarded me with curiosity. "I've never heard that name before. Is it a friend of yours?"

Had I never mentioned Juno to Matteo? That seemed like...an oversight. I realized I hadn't had any sort of contact with Juno since the exhibit.

"Yeah, they're an artist—a painter. Quite flamboyant and eccentric. You'd like them."

"I'd certainly like to meet them at some point." Matteo nodded. "I'll let Vincent know where you've gone."

"Thanks. Charles, leave the keys to your car here. Vincent can drive it back when he's able." I didn't want Charles driving in the agitated state he was in.

I put on my boots and zipped up my jacket, then followed Charles outside.

Luckily, Charles was the kind of mild-mannered boy who did what he was told, even though he had the body of a centerfold, which had doubtless endeared him to Juno initially, although I'd been surprised to hear they were still together. Juno did not have a good track record when it came to relationships. There must be much more to Charles than a pretty smile and a body to die for.

He was subdued during the car ride, although he kept chewing on his blue-polished fingernails—the only not-so-perfect part of him.

"Charles, it's going to be all right."

He shot me a glance that was filled with doubt. "Do you really think so?"

"Have the two of you been having relationship troubles? Or is this coming from out of the blue?"

"Out of the blue. At least, I think so. Juno seemed cheerful enough yesterday."

"Has everything been going well with their art?"

"As far as I know. They were working on a piece they were really excited about...until today."

I shot Charles a glance. "They aren't excited about it anymore?"

Charles shook his head. "This morning, they — they — " Charles rubbed a shaky hand over his eyes. "They destroyed it."

"Oh."

Charles took his bottom lip between his teeth, then released it. "It was a painting of me."

"Oh, sweetie," I said, the endearment coming naturally, even though I barely knew Charles. I examined him as he sat huddled in the car beside me, almost disappearing inside the puffy jacket, his chin down against his chest, his hands clasped in his lap.

"I don't know why they did that," Charles muttered.

I thought I knew what might be going on. Juno had occasional bouts of neuroses, centered around their ability to fulfill their artistic vision. "Juno tends to deal with these sorts of things in a very dramatic way."

"What sorts of things?"

"Self-doubt. Imposter syndrome."

Charles looked confused. "Imposter *what*?"

I shook my head. "It's a thing all artists go through. Most of them go through it *quietly*."

"Huh," Charles said.

"Juno doesn't do anything quietly."

Charles sighed and looked out of the window. "Yeah, I've figured that out."

When we got to the apartment building where they lived, Charles directed me to a Visitor parking spot then took me up to the tenth floor and the apartment he shared with Juno. The building was one of the nicer ones in the city, and the property values at this place must be high. Leave it to Juno to only settle for the best. I'd been here a handful of times, but I realized at that moment that it had been a long time since I'd seen the flamboyant artist.

When Charles keyed us in, he gazed around before moving forward into the empty rooms.

"Charles, Juno's not been physically aggressive with you — or anything?" I asked, because Charles looked wary.

But he shook his head. "No. I just hate to see them so upset and out of control. I don't know what they'll do next — not to me, but to themself or the apartment...or their art. It's hard to...watch."

"Sure." I could understand feeling overwhelmed in a situation like this. I was older and had more experience dealing with eccentric personalities, having hobnobbed with musicians and artists most of my life. I knew Juno and was confident they wouldn't do anything drastic. At least, I didn't think they would.

"They're either in the bedroom or their studio — unless they've gone out," Charles said in low tones, his face pale.

"Okay. Let's check the bedroom first. Why don't you knock and see if you can engage them. I'll be right behind you."

Charles nodded, his face full of worry as he led me to a door past the luxury kitchen. He knocked three times.

"Juno?"

"Go. Away."

Charles glanced at me and swallowed. "I did go away. And now I'm back."

Silence. Then, after a moment, "You should have stayed away."

I tapped Charles' shoulder and indicated he should step back. I rapped the door hard with my knuckles. "Juno. It's Nic. I'd like to come in there."

Silence. Then the soft shuffling of feet sounded, and the doorknob turned slowly. Charles backed up but I stood my ground.

The door cracked open to reveal a disheveled figure who looked somewhat like my friend, Juno. But, since Juno normally didn't show themself to me without a good deal of makeup and over-styled hair, it was difficult to ascertain.

"What do you want?"

Rude. I folded my arms across my chest and raised an imperious eyebrow. "I want to know why you're treating Charles this way. The poor man's about to cry."

A flicker of emotion crossed Juno's face, and their eyes began to shift but then moved back to mine. They licked their lips.

"I don't deserve Charles."

I rolled my eyes. "Let me come in."

Juno glared at me for a long moment, the coldness in their eyes giving me a visceral chill. They'd always been able to project emotional energy with astonishing accuracy and potence.

Poor Charles.

Juno sighed and gave me space to enter, but said, "Charles stays out."

I glanced at the poor man, who was worrying a nail with his teeth.

"Yes, I agree. But don't go anywhere, Charles." I returned my gaze to Juno while speaking to the younger man. "It may not seem like it, but Juno needs you."

Juno narrowed their eyes at me but let me into the room, then closed the door and sank to the floor with their back against it.

It was difficult not to stare. Their haggard appearance was so out-of-character.

They stared at me with a bitterness that surprised me.

"Why did you come?"

"Juno, you're my friend," I said. I gestured to the door. "And poor Charles is so upset."

"He should leave me. I'm no good for him."

I narrowed my eyes. "What's going on?"

Juno made a face. "I'm no good, Nic. Don't you see? I'm no good for anybody."

"Well, you don't look yourself, I'll say that."

"Nobody understands. Nobody values me," Juno muttered, avoiding my gaze.

"That's a little extreme." I sat down on the floor in front of Juno and leaned forward. "What's triggering this? Did something happen?"

Juno sighed. "No, Nic. The problem is, something *didn't* happen."

The plot thickened. "Okay. What *didn't* happen?"

"I didn't get—" Juno sighed again. "The Canadian Council for the Arts rejected my grant proposal."

"Oh. Well, that's too bad. What grant proposal?"

Juno laughed but it wasn't a real laugh. It was a self-deprecating, hopeless spasm.

"The proposal to receive money to support myself while I work on an ambitious project—a project that will now go into the trash as I try to figure out a way to make some money."

I stared at them, confusion swirling through my brain. "I thought you had lots of money." I gazed around us at the opulence of Juno's large bedroom.

"*Had* being the operative word."

"Really? You're serious?" I said. I'd been under the impression that Juno had a somewhat stable and substantial income.

"Oh, Nic, your naiveté as to the fragility of an artist's lifestyle is charming." They met my gaze with a patronizing calm.

"Yes, but...aren't you still selling pieces?"

Juno shrugged. "Once in a while. Demand for my work has gone down."

"Hmm-m. I assumed you were raking in piles of dough." I smiled, but Juno didn't return it.

"Everyone does. And it's fucking embarrassing, to tell the truth." They lowered their voice to a whisper. "Charles and I, we're barely getting by. I hung all my hopes on that grant. And now I'm not getting it, and I don't know what we're going to do."

I ran a hand through my hair, feeling Juno's desperation as if it were my own. "Aw, Juno. I'm sorry."

"Your pity isn't going to pay my bills."

"No, but...I can pay you for that portrait of Vincent and me. How much would you list it for?"

"Twenty-six thousand."

"*What*? Actually?" I was sure they'd quoted me a few thousand when I'd offered to purchase it instead of accepting it as a gift—which they'd insisted upon, because they were my friend.

"No, but that's how much money I need to pay the mortgage fees on this place for the next six months...and the condo fees."

"Juno, I wish I had that money to give you..."

"Well, you don't, Nic. And you can't buy that painting because you can't afford it, and also, it was a gift. It's yours, and I'm not taking it back." Their expression switched from angry to horrified. "Unless you don't want it? Is it that bad? Do you hate it?"

"Juno. Juno, stop. Of course I don't hate it. It's a gorgeous painting and the absolute pride of my home." It was.

"I doubt that's true."

"I don't lie to my friends."

Juno lifted their chin and gazed at me with the most frank and forlorn expression. "Are you my friend, Nic? I haven't seen you in...ages. Not since the gallery show."

Guilt soaked through me at their words, because they were right.

"Well, I—I've been a bit busy, I suppose." Heat filled my cheeks.

"With your charming, beautiful Vincent and the Italian cook. I know. I heard all about it from Daphne," Juno said. "Nothing from you, Nic."

I nodded, unable to meet Juno's honest gaze, feeling terrible for not having reached out over the past several months. I fiddled with a crease in my jeans. "We're also raising a teenager. Did Daphne tell you that?"

"Sparky, you mean? Yes, I've met him. He was at Daphne's one time when I'd gone over there. Delightful boy. Is he a handful?"

"What? No."

"Then why haven't you called?"

Oh, fuck. "I don't— I guess I assumed you were busy with Charles and making art—and hobnobbing with the elite."

Juno's mouth twisted. "The elite. Those nasty fucks."

I moved over and sat down beside them, leaning against the door and staring at their bedroom. The furniture was elegant and feminine, with throw pillows in jeweled tones on every plush surface. "Juno, I'm very sorry I haven't reached out."

"It's all right, Nic. I know I'm stupid and dramatic and entirely fucking useless to anyone. Charles should collect his things and run far, far away from me."

I glared at them, frustrated and angry now. "You don't mean that."

"I don't...care." But their breath hitched, and they had to force the words out. "He's better off without me. I thought I could support him, so he left his job as an interpreter. And now we're fucked."

Oh, good Lord. Juno's life was a mess. But that was no reason to give up and throw away everything they'd worked for.

"I'm sure Charles can get another job," I said.

Juno's expression became hopeless. "Then I've truly failed, haven't I? Can't even be a proper Sugar Daddy."

I couldn't help it, but those words and Juno's vivid reality combined to cause me to snort a laugh.

"Um, Sugar Person," I corrected.

Juno regarded me with disbelief for a long moment. Then the corner of their mouth twitched.

"Honey Mummy?" I suggested.

The lip twitch turned into a grin.

"Candy Aunty?" they offered.

"Oh, that's a good one."

For the first time, Juno seemed like they might not be devising ways to hurt themself or someone else.

"I know things look bleak right now, but, Juno" — I took their hand, threaded their dainty fingers with mine and thumbed at the door behind us — "that despondent boy out there? I'm pretty sure he loves you. And whatever you think of yourself or your talent at the moment, you need to give him the respect of taking him at his word. He *loves* you, and he doesn't want to leave you. And he is stressed as hell right now thinking that you don't love him, thinking that you don't care if he stays or goes. Or that you actually *want* him to go."

"I don't," Juno whispered.

"Well, now we're getting somewhere." I squeezed their hand. "Then stop telling him to leave."

Juno was quiet for a long time. "I don't know how to live up to his expectations of me."

"What do you think his expectations are?"

"That I...take care of him and give him everything he wants, like a proper Sugar Da— I mean, Candy Aunty."

"You think if he finds out you don't have the money to keep him as your pet, he's going to hate you and leave you, so you might as well chase him off?"

Juno mumbled something.

"Pardon?"

"It sounds stupid when you say it."

"It *is* stupid. Why don't you ask Charles what he wants?"

Their head swung around, and they gaped at me. "What? But, how can I do that? What if what he says he wants is...impossible?"

"Juno"—I thumbed at the door again—"that extraordinary young man came all the way to get me because he was worried you were going to hurt yourself, and he didn't understand why you were mad at him. I'm pretty sure all he wants is some reassurance."

Juno put their face in their hands. "Oh, Nic. I keep fucking everything up."

I gently extricated my hand and squeezed their knee.

"Well, this is one thing you can un-fuck right now. I'm calling Charles in, and you're going to tell him everything you've told me. And I'm staying in the room to make sure you aren't treating him like crap. You are an amazing, talented, wonderful person, Juno, but I swear sometimes your head gets stuck so far up your ass it's positively obscene."

"Fine. Get him."

"Okay." I squeezed Juno's knee again to soften the blow of all the hard truths I was dropping and to let them know I felt for them. Then I pushed myself up as Juno stood and went to sit on the edge of the enormous bed. I opened the door and stepped out, searching the flat for Charles, who was nowhere in my sightline.

"Charles?" I called.

He emerged from another room with a dish towel and a stressed-out expression on his cherub-like face. "Yes?"

"Juno wants to talk to you."

Charles hesitated. "I'm just doing the dishes. Probably the mess is what's stressing them out."

I could tell the poor guy had been traumatized by Juno's harsh words.

I walked over to him, took the dish towel from his hand and put it on the table. Then I took both his hands in mine and met his gaze, speaking in low, intimate tones.

"Juno's going through some severe imposter syndrome and self-doubt right now. They don't think they deserve you, so they were intentionally being mean so you'd leave, because they thought that would be best."

Charles seemed to be about to cry. "But I don't want to leave."

"Of course not. And Juno doesn't want that, either. I've explained that their mind was playing tricks on them, and I've given them reassurance that they are *not* a terrible artist, and they are worthy of you still. Did you know about the Canadian Council of the Arts proposal?"

Charles blinked and frowned like a confused puppy. "The *what*?"

"Never mind. Juno can explain. The gist of it is that they are working on a project involving you, planning to devote all their artistic energies to creating art *devoted* to you, and now they don't know how they're going to pay the bills because a grant fell through that would have supported both of you while Juno worked on it."

"Oh."

"And, it's also my fault. I've neglected our friendship, and I feel awful about that."

Charles nodded. "I wondered why you never came over. Juno talks about you all the time."

"They do?" I said, surprised.

"Yeah. And Vincent, too."

"Oh fuck. I'm so sorry, Charles." I ran a hand through my hair, suddenly feeling like shit. "I've been a bit busy but mostly self-absorbed the past little while."

Charles nodded, as if to dismiss my apology. He didn't seem to care about my excuses. He just wanted Juno to feel better. "Do they want to talk to me? Really?"

"Yes, they do…really." It was Juno's voice.

We looked over to see Juno making their way over to where we stood near the kitchen. Charles stood still as Juno approached and took his sweet face between their delicate hands. They gazed into Charles' eyes.

"I am so sorry. Nothing can excuse my behavior toward you. I don't even know if you can forgive – ?"

"I forgive you," Charles said, a single tear emerging from the corner of his eye and trailing across his rosy cheek.

"Oh, darling…" Juno said, their voice breaking. They came together in a tentative embrace. I averted my gaze and picked up the dish towel.

"I'll finish drying the dishes," I said, and left them to their reunion.

In the kitchen, I pulled out my phone and sent a text to Vincent and Matteo, explaining that everything was okay but that I was staying a bit longer and would be home later that evening. I'd have to explain that we needed to make an effort to include Juno and Charles in our lives from this point forward. We'd been neglectful of our friends, and it couldn't continue.

I sighed and got to work in the kitchen. It was a bit of a disaster, but with focus and hard work, I had it back to being presentable in about half an hour. I folded the towel neatly and placed it on the clean counter. When I went back into the main room, Charles and

Juno had gone, and suspicious sounds came from the bedroom. Good sounds.

Then knocking came on the apartment door. I opened it to Vincent.

"Hey," I said, pulling him into my arms.

"How's Juno?"

"Better. But I feel like shit. We've been neglecting Juno...and Charles. We're supposed to be their friends."

Vincent hugged me close. "Charles' car is parked in Visitors." He handed me the keys.

I put them on the side table and wrote out a note, using the pen and paper that was there.

I'm so sorry I've neglected you, Juno. Please bring Charles to dinner Saturday. You need to meet Matteo and Taylor properly, and we need to reconnect. Charles' car is in Visitors. XO.
Nic

I explained everything to Vincent on the drive home.

* * * *

"Nic, how are things with Juno and Charles?" Matteo said as soon as he saw us.

I sat on the sofa beside him, tugging Vincent down next to me.

"Better. But, uh, it seems I've been remiss in my personal obligations. Would you mind cooking for six people on Saturday?"

Matteo shook his head. "Not at all. I can do spaghetti Bolognese. That's a delicious and straightforward dish."

"Thank you. That would be wonderful."

I explained about the grant that Juno had missed out on, and how that and my neglect had initiated a spiral into self-doubt and worry about finances.

"Poor Juno," Vincent murmured. "Their art is so beautiful!"

"Yes, it is. I offered to buy that painting they gave us, but Juno wouldn't hear of it. They also said they'd charge me twenty-six thousand bucks for it, which I don't have. Not as disposable funds, anyway."

"Whoa," Vincent said.

"Yeah, whoa. I have no doubt they've sold some of their art for at least a few thousand. I'm not saying that painting isn't worth twenty K, but, I guess... I don't know."

Matteo frowned. "Maybe we could offer to organize an exhibit? Help them sell some pieces? Could we incorporate some kink into an art show? Maybe have some demos, human display pieces, that sort of thing?"

It didn't take much effort to picture it. We could invite the elites—nasty fucks though they might be—who would come for the titillation and hopefully leave with an art piece for their dungeon.

"That...is not a half bad idea," I said, tapping my chin.

* * * *

Plans for the event began to materialize. We would call it *Electric Dreams – An Erotic Illusion.*

There would be an attendance fee, and we located a space we could use for a minimal rental price. The many connections I'd made over the years in the Ottawa kink community meant we had all kinds of volunteers to help. We decided to keep it casual, like Matteo had suggested — something a little kinkier than your average gallery show.

I made a list of all the elite kinksters, intellectuals and artists I knew in town, even those who might not buy a painting. Because an event was only as good as its participants, and I truly wanted people to enjoy themselves. Besides, happy attendees were more likely to go home with a painting or two.

Between Vincent and I, we had the entire event pretty well organized by the time Juno and Charles arrived on Saturday.

Now we simply had to sell *them* on the idea.

"A gallery exhibit? In my honor?" Juno said, their hand going to their heart. They were wearing the most avant-garde bespoke suit that somehow managed to be formal and flirty at the same time, with a crisp white blouse underneath the blue brocade vest.

"Well, that was the idea. Matteo came up with it, really."

Juno turned to my partners and smiled, a gleam in their intelligent eyes. "I see. And will Matteo and Vincent be part of the demo portion of this event?"

Vincent blushed, and Matteo smiled.

Juno clapped their hands together. "Excellent. I think it's a capital idea." They turned to Charles, who looked much recovered from the last time I'd seen him. "What do you think, darling?"

"It sounds wonderful," Charles admitted. He'd worn a pair of slim, burgundy jeans with a black button-down and gray vest. No jacket. "Do you think Juno will sell some of their work?"

"I'm counting on it," I said. "We're going to let people know that the pieces won't be available anywhere else. And we'd like to sell them at a slight discount."

"A discount?" Juno gasped. "You mean…on *sale*?"

Charles sent a worried glance Juno's way, then turned to me in desperation.

I came in with some damage control.

"Look, Juno. You need to sell some work. In most circumstances, when people need to sell stock in a hurry, it's marked down."

Juno went very pale and clutched the arm of my chair for support. "Marked…*down*? Like at some *bargain basement* supply store?"

Matteo, bless his heart, intervened. "No, of course not. Call it *an exclusive offer* to the participants of this… *very prestigious* event."

Juno took a breath. "That sounds — better… marginally." They sent another glare my way.

Charles seemed relieved. "Juno, you know you have so many pieces. And all they're doing right now is sitting in the apartment, where nobody can see them."

"True. Very true," Juno said, reaching out to take Charles' hand.

"It might be nice to show them off to people who can appreciate your incredible talent," Vincent added.

Juno smiled, and I felt grateful to Vincent for kowtowing to the temperamental and sensitive artist. "Vincent, you have a silver tongue in that gorgeous mouth of yours," they said.

They looked at Charles, then back at Vincent.

"I have often fantasized about putting Vincent and Charles together in some sort of scene. Perhaps a shibari suspension or some such thing. Maybe we could discuss that, Nic, for this event?"

I would be lying if I said that the thought of suspending Vincent and Charles together from the ceiling, naked and wrapped in brightly colored ropes, didn't thrill me, but I held my enthusiasm in check for the time being. I wasn't sure that a display of such grandiosity was going to be possible.

"We can discuss it with Vincent and Charles, I suppose," I said. "But only if you agree to participate in this event, Juno, and to offer some of your pieces for display and sale."

Juno contemplated for a moment, then gave a long-suffering sigh. "I suppose I can do that, since you all have your hearts set on this."

"Excellent. Now let's go eat the spaghetti Matteo has made and, afterward, we can retire to the living room for some expensive brandy."

"A wonderful idea, Nic," Juno said. "I could use a drink."

"Fair enough."

Now that Juno had accepted the idea of the exhibit, Charles smiled and said, "It sounds like so much fun. I think it's a great idea!"

Juno regarded their young boyfriend with benign amusement. "Oh, Charles. My mind is already spinning with ideas for how to display you."

Charles' face flushed and his lips parted.

Juno's smile widened. "You are going to be an important part of this exhibit. Perhaps even the star attraction."

Charles fought a smile. "Anything for you. You know that."

Juno slid a hand to Charles' slim neck and brought him close for a kiss to the cheek. "I do know that, my love."

Chapter Three

Taylor had a few things to say about Juno's predicament.

"We need to start a GoFundMe."

"A what?" Matteo asked.

Taylor laughed. "It's a way to get people to give you money online, old man."

Matteo looked skeptical. "Is that legal?"

Taylor rolled his eyes. "*Yes,* it's legal. People do it all the time."

I glanced at our resident tech and social media expert. "Hmm. Can you set one up?"

"Sure. I can start one today, if you want."

"I'll have to ask Juno. Will they know what that is?"

Taylor shrugged. "Probably? How old *is* Juno?"

That gave me pause. Things like age and gender didn't mean a hell of a lot when it came to Juno.

"I think they're in their early thirties. It's hard to know because I have a funny feeling they might lie about their age."

"If that's remotely accurate, they'd know about it." Taylor took the carton of milk from the fridge and poured himself a tumbler full.

"Easy. We're going through a lot of milk these days, Taylor," I said.

He grinned and raised the glass. "I'm a growing boy," he said, before tipping it to his lips and drinking.

"Hmm. I might have to raise your rent."

He carried the glass into the living room, giving me a smirk. He knew I wouldn't raise his rent. He was already paying us a decent monthly amount—enough to cover most of his grocery needs. But I enjoyed teasing him about how much he seemed to eat and drink—like a parent, I supposed.

Taylor had a part-time job at the local GLBTQ+ shelter, and he was applying to college programs for social work. He wanted to help kids like him, who had been forced to leave their family homes because of discrimination and emotional or physical abuse. He'd been hired for clerical duties and was the person at the front desk. So, he already interacted with the people who needed the shelter's services, but he wanted to be more qualified in order to assist them.

"Oh, by the way, I'm also helping Daphne set up an OnlyFans account. I can't believe she doesn't have one. She can make so much more money than she does already."

Vincent shook his head. "I hate to say it, but that's genius, Taylor. You're probably right."

"I know I'm right. But she didn't even know what it was, so it's been interesting...uh...introducing her to the concept." He glanced at the rest of us. "Everyone knows about OnlyFans, at least?"

Matteo threw up his hands. "I'm afraid not."

Taylor turned my way. "Nic. Come on!"

I smiled blithely. "Oh, I might know a little bit about OnlyFans."

Taylor opened his mouth, and his eyes widened. "You don't—? You don't have—?"

"Oh, for God's sake. No, I don't have an OnlyFans, Taylor." I ran my index finger along the edge of the coffee table. "I might…just follow some accounts."

Taylor smiled, then laughed, then choked on his laughter and sat down beside me, fixing me with a panicked stare. "Okay, just don't…um, follow sparkytreats19, for *all that is holy…*"

"Oh, for God's sake." I exchanged a look with Vincent, who seemed equally horrified. "Are you serious right now? Is it photos or videos? I suppose I shouldn't be surprised."

Taylor at least had the grace to go all red in the face. "I have my pup hood on the whole time."

"You mean, *my* pup hood," Vincent said.

Taylor narrowed his eyes at his cousin. "I thought you were a *cat.*"

"Meow," Matteo said, with a glint of humor in his eyes. "I don't know what all this is about, but something tells me you are sharing racy videos…with someone?" He glanced at Vincent and me for corroboration, but we could only regard him with pity.

"Exactly," Taylor said, with a smirk. "But they can't identify me. At least, not by my…face."

"Well, that's something," I said. "I don't really want to talk about this anymore."

"Neither do I," Vincent said. "Although I do admit getting Daphne an OnlyFans account is a good idea."

"Thank you," Taylor said. "But explaining to her how to use it and how to upload stuff is a nightmare."

"Oh, I'll bet. Daphne doesn't like to be an ingenue. She likes to be in control."

"Yeah. Well, for now, I'm kind of her technical director, videographer and social media manager. I've got her up on all the relevant platforms. She's kind of getting the hang of Facebook, hates Twitter with a passion, and so far, I'm managing her Instagram."

"She should pay you. That's a lot of work, Taylor."

He shrugged. "She's my friend. I'm helping her out."

I nodded. "Right. But she's getting a lot of your time for free."

"I don't mind. Riley helps. He thinks it's a hoot."

"Well, that's good. Now, do you mind giving Matteo and Vincent and me some privacy? I want to discuss this gallery show we're planning."

"Sure. But, wait. Can Riley and me go?"

"If you buy tickets, I suppose so. But I am not apologizing for anything you might observe at this event." I glanced at Vincent, who went quite red in the face.

"But...it's an art show."

"It's a kinky art show."

"Of course it fucking is. How kinky?"

"There may be naked people."

"I think we can handle that."

"Used as furniture."

"Oh?"

"Or bound with rope in compromising positions."

Taylor cocked his head. "Sounds like an evening at Daphne's place. We'll be there."

"I figured."

Taylor went upstairs, and I turned to Matteo and Vincent, bringing my hands together. "So, I have some ideas for *Electric Dreams*. Would you like to hear them?"

Matteo turned his gaze from the muted television screen and smiled, while Vincent snuggled up close to me and said, "Naked furniture?"

I took his hand in mine.

"Have you ever been used as a serving platter?"

"Never," he said. His blue eyes went wide, and he shuddered.

I smiled, quite benignly. "Only if you're into it. Think about it, please."

Vincent glanced at Matteo, who seemed intent on Vincent's answer.

"I want to."

"You sure?"

"Well, all I have to do is lie there, right? Nobody's going to touch me inappropriately or anything?"

"No, Vincent, I'm not letting anyone touch you. We will ensure that our guests abide by strict rules of conduct. Don't worry."

He nodded, then flushed and squirmed.

"Are you hard just thinking about it?"

"Yes."

"Well, well, well, a serving platter with an erection. I can't wait to see it."

Vincent went even redder at the thought of it. "Oh, God."

"I'll probably cage you, because an erection of your" —I glanced at the bulge in his pants— "*stature* might be distracting for our guests."

"Oh," he said, and it was almost a moan.

"It will be challenging. You're going to have to lie as still as you can, for at least thirty minutes. Maybe sixty. I haven't decided yet."

His forehead wrinkled. "I didn't think about that. What if I get an itch?"

I shrugged. "Well, you'll have two choices. Move and risk the food falling off, or tough it out and be the exquisite piece of living furniture I know you can be." I leaned in and kissed him. "With any luck, you won't be alone. I'm going to ask Charles to serve as well. If he's willing, we could have two tables, or one large table, if we put the two of you together somehow."

"Oh my goodness," Matteo said.

I met his dark gaze. "Right?"

"And what would you like me to do?" Matteo asked.

"Why, prepare the food that will adorn our two beautiful slaves, of course. And also, walk around in a tuxedo and serve champagne."

"Of course, Sir."

Matteo's gaze met Vincent's.

* * * *

I had Charles visit me at work the next day. I wanted to check in with him anyway, and it was convenient to speak in the privacy of my office. It was only a ten-minute walk from their apartment.

Charles seemed pleased to see my office. I swept my hand in a grand gesture at the modest space, strewn with papers and random objects. "I contemplated asking Vincent to organize it for me, but that would be simply too pitiful and not really fair. He already takes excellent care of our home. I couldn't have him responsible for my workspace as well."

Charles smiled. "It's cozy."

"Yes. Have a seat." I gestured to the wooden armchair in front of my cluttered desk. "I wanted to check in with you. How are things with Juno?"

Charles flushed and scratched his chin, where a light shadow of stubble was visible. It looked good on him—

usually he was clean shaven. "Much better. They're back to their"—Charles tilted his head and raised his eyebrows—"normal level of..." He shrugged and laughed, as if he couldn't think of a word to describe Juno's regular state of being.

I laughed too. "I get you. Well, that's good to hear."

"Thank you, Nic. You, Vincent and Matteo—and Taylor, as well—have been so helpful. And now Juno knows they have friends who will stand by them."

I frowned. "Yes. I'm going to make sure they continue to know that. It's not fair for you to shoulder all the responsibility for Juno's happiness." I put my chin in my hands. "They've always been a little on the high needs end of things. It can be exhausting if it's not spread about."

Charles regarded me with a frankness and confidence I found reassuring.

"I love them so much," he said. "As soon as I met them, I knew I wanted to be, somehow, important to them." He shrugged. "I'm pretty sure I was simply a boy-toy for a month or so. Then, every time I was convinced Juno was going to say they'd had enough of me, they surprised me by keeping me close. And soon, I realized we were falling for each other. I still can't believe it, half the time."

"I think you are good for Juno. And I think they are lucky to have you."

Charles blinked quickly and nodded. "Thank you. It means a lot."

"Now, look... I have a crazy idea for this art exhibit. Would you be willing to serve as a living food platter? You know, lie on a table and have food displayed on you, for guests to sample?"

Charles smiled. "Sure."

I squinted at him. "Have you done this before?"

"No, but I've always wanted to try it."

"I've asked Vincent as well. The two of you will make quite the statement, while being perfectly quiet and obedient."

"Oh!" Charles agreed. "Has Vincent done it before?"

I shook my head and smiled. "Never. It will be quite the experience for you both. Are you comfortable being caged, Charles?"

Charles blanched. "Um. You're going to put me in a cage?"

I laughed, although it was an understandable interpretation of what I'd said. "No, no, I mean, I'm going to put your *cock* in a cage."

Charles blinked. "What?" His eyes widened and his lips parted.

"For the event. Not right now."

Charles seemed to scramble for some mental purchase. "Oh. I don't know. I've never...what exactly does that mean? Is it — painful?"

I grinned. "Only if you become aroused."

He frowned. "Oh." He looked like he was going to say something else, but didn't.

"I don't have to cage you, darling Charles. Only I think you would look lovely all vulnerable and restrained by a metal device on your privates."

His forehead creased. "Will Vincent be...caged...also?"

"Oh yes. He would prefer to be caged than fully erect, as that would be conspicuous and embarrassing."

"Oh, right."

"But it's your choice, Charles. I think that Juno would appreciate how lovely you're going to look, although I don't doubt you'd look gorgeous *without* a cock cage."

"Sure. I can try it, I guess." He didn't seem convinced.

I put a comforting hand on his shoulder. "Look… I'll touch base with Juno about this, because I want to make sure they're okay with it. And maybe they could try putting you in one for a few hours or a couple of days—"

Charles' eyes went wide as saucers. "A couple of *days*?"

I laughed. "Trust me. It's not as brutal as it sounds. I'll have Vincent give you a call and explain the concept a bit more."

"Okay."

"Honestly, Charles, it's one of Vincent's favorite things."

"If you say so."

When I told Juno what I had proposed for the event, they agreed that Vincent and Charles serving as living food platters would be an intriguing addition to the decor.

"Nic, would it be possible for us to come over to, um, give Charles a glimpse into the experience of being caged? He's never expressed any interest, but I think he might like it."

"I'm not sure what you mean."

"Well, I think that if Charles can see that Vincent acts normal, even though his cock is behind bars, it will put him at ease about the whole thing."

"Well, I supposed that depends on Vincent," I said.

* * * *

A few days later, Vincent agreed to have Charles and Juno visit while he was under lock and key.

Juno seemed to have regained their mental footing, wearing a gorgeous sweater in aquamarine with a cowl neck, tight black jeans and a pair of ankle boots. They'd lined their eyes and contoured their cheeks, which was an improvement. Not that I cared, but at least they'd put in the effort to look the way they liked. That said a lot about their mental state.

At my suggestion, they'd also resumed monthly counseling sessions with a trusted practitioner who specialized in helping people with coping strategies for anxiety and overwhelm. They were queer and kink positive, which enabled Juno to be open and trusting with them. It was vital that Juno had this support, as it shouldn't fall to Charles and the rest of us to maintain Juno's mental health, although we'd do our best to support it.

Vincent had dressed in his favorite pair of purple sweatpants with 'Princess' scrawled across the backside, opting for a less dressy option in the interests of demonstrating how casual and comfortable a cock cage could be. There was no need for Vincent to get naked for everyone, although he would if I asked. I wanted Charles to see how unobtrusive a cock cage could be — in case, you know, he decided to wear one for a longer period of time at any point. I had a feeling that once he'd been in one for the event, he'd be begging Juno to lock him up.

"Are you wearing it now?" Charles asked, staring at Vincent's crotch.

"Yeah."

"I can't even tell."

"Stand up, Vincent," I said.

My obedient boy stood.

"Hands behind your back, please."

He obeyed. I moved in behind him and gathered the purple fabric at his hips, pulling it snug so Juno and

Charles could see the hard outlines of the metal cage over Vincent's privates.

"Oh! I see," Charles commented. "That's...wow."

"He's flaccid, of course." I peeked inside the waistband of Vincent's pants, then let the elastic snap back. "Well, mostly. That's the point," I said.

Charles blushed and slid his hands nervously along his thighs.

"I really want to see it," he said, glancing at Vincent with a pleading expression.

"Come on," Vincent said, holding out his hand. "I'll show you, but not in front of these two."

Vincent led Charles to the powder room off the kitchen then closed the door behind them.

"Well, well, well. Fast friends already," Juno commented.

I shrugged. "It's nice for Vincent to have a friend his age. How old is Charles?"

"Oh, Nic. My dear Charles is twenty-four. Much too young for me, don't you know."

"He's perfect for you. Vincent's twenty-five. Well, he'll be twenty-six in a month. God, we're all getting older," I said.

"Perhaps you are." Juno smirked. "I have decided to be thirty-three for the foreseeable future. What is *time*, after all? It's only a human construct."

I raised my brows. "I don't think that's actually true, Juno—"

They tossed their wavy, shoulder length hair. "Humor me, Nic. You usually do."

"Fine."

"At any rate, the two of them make a great pair. Vincent and Charles. I'm looking forward to the gallery show."

"Me, too."

"And where is Matteo this evening?"

"He's upstairs lying down. He's got a bad headache."

"Poor man. I'm sure it's not easy living in such a busy household." Juno shook their head and clicked their tongue. "And Taylor?"

"Taylor is at Daphne's, helping her with clients. Did you know he's setting up an OnlyFans for her?"

"Is he? Such a little entrepreneur. I should ask him to help me with my website. It needs updating, and I don't have the technical skills he does. That boy should get a degree in communications. I imagine there is a great demand for people with his skills."

"He's applied for the Social Work program at Algonquin. That's where his interest lies."

We glanced over as Vincent and Charles returned to the living room. Charles looked flushed, and Vincent seemed agitated.

"What's wrong?" I asked him.

"Nothing." Vincent flashed me a smile.

"I'm an idiot," Charles blurted. "I wanted to touch it and"—his gaze flashed to Vincent—"I should have asked first. I'm so sorry."

"Charles, it's fine. I'm just...a bit uncomfortable now," Vincent said.

I grinned. "Because you're aroused, Vincent?"

He glared at me. "Maybe."

"Don't worry, my darling," Juno said to Charles, tilting his chin up and gazing into Charles' beautiful eyes. "Vincent will forgive you."

Vincent waved them off. "There's nothing to forgive. It's not a big deal. But, just so you know, when you get hard in a cock cage, it's not exactly comfortable."

"But that's part of its charm, isn't it, Vincent?" I said, running a finger over the bulge in his sweats.

Vincent sighed and rested his forehead on my shoulder. "Yes," he murmured.

"So?" Juno asked Charles. "What do you think? Can you handle having your privates locked away to serve me?"

"Probably. Vincent says it makes things easier. You know, that it's harder to have" — Charles cleared his throat — "accidents."

Juno laughed and clapped their hands together. "Well, any assistance in that department would be beneficial. Although I do so love to see you overcome."

The way the two of them regarded each other at that moment reassured me that all was well between them. Juno was lucky that Charles was so forgiving and accommodating. Someone else might have gotten fed up with Juno's dramatic and self-flagellating behavior and left. Perhaps they *were* meant for each other. Charles was the only one of Juno's partners who'd lasted so long, and he seemed to thrive in Juno's company.

After they'd left, I pulled Vincent close and kissed him sweetly on his divine lips. Then I tugged him across my lap and pulled the back of his sweatpants down so that I could see and touch his beautiful behind.

"What are you doing?" he asked breathlessly, staring back at me as I cupped one perfect globe in my hand and jiggled it.

"What does it look like?"

He gasped and made a small stutter of a sound. "Are you punishing me? Did I do something wrong?"

I laughed. "Absolutely not. I'm very pleased with you," I said, wetting a finger and running it along his crack.

Vincent jerked over my lap, the metal cage under his sweats bumping against my leg.

"What are you doing, Sir?" he said, attempting to keep from moaning.

"I'm playing with you. Since Matteo's upstairs and not in any shape to join us, I'm enjoying having you to myself."

"Oh."

I wiggled the tip of my finger against his fluttering hole. Vincent made the most delicious whimpering sound.

"I see you obeyed my instructions about not putting panties on today?"

"Yes, Sir."

"Although I do like you in the frilly underthings you wear, it's also nice to have you go commando."

"Yes, Sir."

"I want to spank you right now, but not for punishment, because you've been very, very *good*."

"But...but I won't be able to come...since I have the cage on," Vincent said, breathing hard and squirming while I teased him with my finger.

"Oh, that's true. What a shame," I said, evincing not a shred of concern.

"It's going to get me so horny. I'm already so, so horny."

"I know."

"Ah, fuck," Vincent said. "Whatever you wish, Sir."

"Give me your left wrist. I want to keep you in place."

Vincent brought his wrist to his lower back and I grabbed it, bending his arm at the elbow and holding him firmly. I pushed against his hole a little more, then brought my hand up and brought it down lightly on his cheeks.

"Ow," he said.

"That didn't fucking hurt."

He huffed a laugh. "No, Sir."

"Then why did you say 'ow'?"

"Acting?"

Now I was the one who laughed. "Oh, all right. We're going to be funny today, are we? Let's see how funny this is, my dear." I tugged his sweatpants down to his knees.

I began to spank him, not harshly, but in a way I knew would push any tendencies to humor from Vincent's mind. I spanked him the way he liked best, the way I knew would make him horny as fuck, the way I liked to spank him when I wanted him to rut on my leg and overflow.

Only right now he couldn't. And I don't think he thought it was funny anymore.

I'd spank him just hard enough that he'd feel it and light enough that the pain wouldn't overshadow the way he felt about *being* spanked, over my knee, in the living room, solely because I wanted to do it and didn't give a fuck that he wouldn't be able to come.

Thank God Taylor was at Daphne's and Matteo was indisposed. Because this was about *my* pleasure, and Vincent's enjoyment came second to that—and maybe not at all.

After about ten minutes, I could tell he was suffering, and it wasn't from the pain of the spanking, although his ass had pinked up nicely. He moaned with each strike and the cage bumped my leg. My jeans were getting wet from the amount of pre-ejaculate he was producing. This was all going very well to plan.

I stopped and rubbed my hand over the heated swell of his buttock, then wet my other finger and dipped it between his cheeks again. When the tip made contact with his hole, Vincent cried out.

"No, no, no," he panted, trying to squirm away. I held him firm.

"Your safeword is 'stitches', if you forgot." I continued to press against his hole.

"I didn't!"

"Then stay still and let me play with you."

Vincent made a sound like a sigh or a sob and went limp.

"Yes, Sir," he said, voice ragged, and I mentally congratulated myself on a job well done. But it wasn't over yet.

Taking my time, I pushed my finger slowly, tortuously, into Vincent's ass as he made the most defeated sound and shuddered with desire—desire that he had no hope of releasing.

"Good boy," I said, wiggling my finger as Vincent whimpered.

He froze as I adjusted the position of my hand so my finger stroked over his prostate.

Vincent made a strangled sound.

"Oh, boy, I bet that feels good. I want to keep you in this state of frustrated arousal for the rest of the evening."

"Oh, Sir," he groaned, giving himself up to me and my wishes, like the obedient boy he was. In the end, I'd let him pull up his pants. Then I'd made him stand by the sofa and watch me masturbate myself to orgasm at least three times, until he was a trembling wreck of a man who could barely think straight.

Then, even though I'd made him imagine he'd be in this state all night, I unlocked the cage and pulled it off, then went to my knees and took his poor, leaking cock in my mouth. He came in less than a minute, choking me on massive amounts of jizz as he cried out, struggling to keep his hands behind his back.

I swallowed it all, then stood and took his dear face between my palms and kissed him long and slow and dreamy, until he melted against me and begged me to take him to bed, after thanking me for the privilege of being exquisitely tortured.

Chapter Four

Matteo's headache had gone by the time we woke the next day. He had cuddled up with Vincent in the night and now they were both awake and canoodling beside me.

"Somebody got out of their cage, I see," Matteo said, his hand moving under the blankets in the vicinity of Vincent's groin.

"Not until Nic had tortured me over his lap for an hour," Vincent muttered in a contented tone I knew all too well.

Matteo chuckled.

"It wasn't an hour," I said, yawning and moving in behind Matteo, who felt warm and smelled lovely. "How's your head?"

"Fine now. Thank you for letting me rest undisturbed yesterday evening."

"No worries. I kept Vincent very entertained downstairs."

Matteo glanced at Vincent who squirmed at the memory. "Yes, it sounds like it."

Vincent groaned and side-eyed Matteo. "What are you doing?"

"I'm playing with your morning erection," Matteo commented blithely. "Would you like me to stop?"

"Never."

I grabbed the blankets, whipping them off the mischievous pair in one motion, then propped my head on my elbow and peered down at the action. "At least let me watch."

"Of course, Sir," Matteo murmured, giving Vincent's hard cock lazy strokes.

Vincent rolled onto his back to allow Matteo more access and me a better view. He sighed and moaned, at peace with a wake-up hand job after having been caged the whole day previous.

I kissed Matteo on the shoulder. "Make it good, Matteo. He's going back into lock-up after breakfast."

"Of course, Sir," Matteo replied as I got up and out of bed.

Vincent moaned, and I didn't have to look back to know he was fake-pouting. "But why?"

"Because it's good for a boy to know who his Master is, who controls him." I lifted my hand and clenched it into a tight fist, winking at my lovely submissive. "Who holds all of his pleasure in one hand."

Matteo chuckled and bent to take Vincent's cock into his mouth as I entered the en suite to a long, low groan.

* * * *

Vincent enjoyed giving me absolute control over his orgasms. He enjoyed pleasing me, he enjoyed denial and, really, he enjoyed the process of becoming more and more aroused over a period of a few days, until he started to go out of his mind with it. The build-up of desire and need and want was a heady feeling, I supposed, and a powerful, mind-bending orgasm when I released him was worth the time in captivity.

I very much enjoyed holding the key to Vincent's satisfaction. Or, on occasion, such as this one, I gave Matteo the honor. We were trying to switch things up as Daphne had suggested, and Matteo was more than willing to take control of our boy.

"Of course, Sir. I do not take this honor lightly," Matteo said, taking the tiny key from me while Vincent looked on with interest.

I turned to him. "Don't think you can use your wicked wiles on Matteo to get that thing off before I approve it. He still has to go through me."

Vincent rolled his eyes.

"Hmm-m. That's an extra few hours I've just added."

Vincent frowned. "I'm sorry, Sir."

"I'm sure you are."

"Sir—"

I raised my eyebrows, shutting him up. "You aren't starting off very well. Let Matteo choose a pair of panties for you to wear and get yourself dressed."

"Yes, Sir."

"We're going to Daphne's for tea this afternoon, so make sure they are very pretty and very lacy, Matteo. She'll want him to strip."

"Yes, Sir."

"And wear some nice boxer briefs yourself. She may want you both to serve her."

"Of course."

We hadn't been to tea at Daphne's in ages, and she had invited us around this weekend. I was hoping to let her in on everything happening with Juno and give her an idea of the event we were planning. She should be able to provide a list of people to invite, on top of the names I already had written down.

* * * *

"Taylor! Get your ass down here if you want a ride to Daphne's," I yelled upstairs.

Daphne had requested we bring her 'technical advisor' with us, although she'd sworn she'd keep him busy in her office while we enjoyed afternoon tea in the living room.

"Be there in a minute!" he called down.

When Taylor came downstairs, he grabbed his jacket and shoved his feet into his boots. "Okay, let's go. I hope Daphne has those little egg salad sandwiches she had last time."

I crooked an eyebrow. "She probably will, but they will be served by Vincent in frilly panties."

Taylor shrugged. "Nothing fazes me anymore, Nic. Those sandwiches are worth it. Oh, and the marshmallow puffs! She knows I love those."

I laughed, Matteo grinned and Vincent shook his head. We piled into the car. Vincent drove, as usual. I spent the time wondering what kind of tiny little sandwiches Daphne would serve and what lingerie Matteo had dressed Vincent in.

Snowflakes fluttered down from above like we were in a kinky snowglobe.

Daphne greeted us at the door and waved us in with a big grin. "Come inside! Come inside. Hiya, Sparky. I've got lots of work for you today."

Taylor smiled. "Can I still have tea and cookies?"

"Of course!"

Taylor headed for the office in the back of the house as Daphne greeted the rest of us. "Hello, Vincent, Matteo, Nic."

"Hello, Daphne. Are you paying Taylor for his assistance?" I asked.

She took my coat. "Yes, Nic. We have agreed on a modest hourly wage. I thought you didn't want me to pay him for the work he did for me?"

"Well, not for that— Never mind. But if he's doing technical, computer stuff, he should get something out of it. That's a marketable skill."

"So is what I do."

"I know, but—"

She held up her hand. "I know, I know. You would like Taylor to explore other avenues of work before he ends up in the sex trade. Typical parent."

"Yes, well, I am not a typical parent, but I still want the best for my...child." Taylor wasn't a child, and he wasn't legally mine, but he felt like my kid. "And unfortunately, sex work is still not a respected field, and I don't want him to come up against even more discrimination than he'll face for being gay."

"Yes, I agree. And while I value his assistance in my dungeon and I think he has an affinity for that kind of work, it took me a long time to build up enough clientele to make this a workable 'career'. So, I do agree with you."

"Oh. Good."

Matteo, who had taken off his coat, embraced Daphne and kissed her cheek. "How are you, Mistress Daphne?"

"Fantastic, now that you're here." Daphne gestured to a tallish man, who had just entered the room. "All of you, this is Alexander. Alexander, these are Nic, Vincent and Matteo, my dear friends."

"Alexander," I said, offering my hand. "Delighted to meet you. Nic Walker.

Alexander nodded and cleared his throat. "Likewise."

He was taller than me, and slim, with salt-and-pepper hair and a close-cropped beard. *Very handsome.* But, of course he would be. Daphne didn't fuck ugly men, so she definitely wouldn't fall in love with one. I only hoped Alexander's heart matched his outward appearance.

The others exchanged pleasantries, and we moved into the living room.

"Are we having tea in here?" I asked, since we usually sat at the kitchen table.

"But of course!" Daphne said. "Since there are so many of us."

Daphne's living room decor consisted of a plethora of leather pieces, including a full couch and a love seat. These pieces were of classic design, rather than the popular but hideously over-stuffed reclining options. They were studded with metal along the edges and featured wooden arms with elaborate scroll work.

There was a leather armchair, also, and a large antique chest in place of a coffee table.

"Nic and Alexander, make yourselves comfortable. Vincent and Matteo, come along. I'll show you what you'll be serving our guests."

My partners followed Daphne into the kitchen, and I found myself alone with Alexander.

I leaned forward with my elbows on my knees. "Do you prefer Alexander or Alex?"

He shrugged. "Either is fine. My pronouns are he/him."

"Awesome. Mine are he/him, as well."

We were silent for a moment. Then Alexander turned a sharp-eyed gaze my way. "Do you mind if I ask how long the three of you have been together?"

"Not at all. Vincent and I have been together for about a year, and Matteo got pulled into the relationship about six months ago."

He smiled. "I love to see people living their lives the way they want to and not the way society dictates they should."

"Yes, well, I learned at a young age that if I wanted to be happy, I needed to disregard what society was telling me about myself and simply do what I wanted."

"You are a very interesting person, Nic. You radiate a confidence and energy that is undeniable. If I didn't already know you were a Dominant, I would know it from the distinct way you have about you."

"Thank you...I think." I laughed.

"It's a compliment. I think you are fascinating."

"Oh. Well, thanks. I'm feeling pretty fucking ordinary these days, but okay. Now that I'm guiding an eighteen-year-old through the first delicate stages of adulthood, I find myself thoroughly domesticated."

Alexander laughed and it made his eyes crinkle at the edges. "No doubt. But you're...lifestyle...seems far from domesticated to me."

"So...you and Daphne, huh?" I wanted to get the focus off me.

Alexander blushed. "She's quite something."

I laughed. "She certainly is." I didn't know exactly what Daphne had told Alexander, so I didn't expand on what I knew. But I was pleased to see him here, because whatever she had said to him about her feelings, it seemed that he might just return them. He certainly wouldn't be here meeting us if he were only a client, and if he'd found a new Domme, he definitely wouldn't be here hobnobbing with Daphne's friends.

Just then, Daphne breezed into the room carrying a pile of napkins.

"Tea is served!" she announced as she placed the serviettes on the antique chest as Vincent and Matteo appeared, carrying trays with the pot of tea, an assortment of fancy teacups and milk and sugar.

"Holy fuck," I said.

Daphne—it must have been her handiwork—had dressed Vincent in a powder blue, satin Maid's dress, complete with short, ruffled sleeves and white apron. His long legs were encased in black stockings and the edges of the garter straps holding them up peeked out from the skirt. On his feet were platform Mary Jane shoes with a low heel.

"Good lord!" Alexander commented. "You look adorable, Vincent."

Vincent placed the tray carefully down on the coffee table, stood and, taking the edges of the skirt in his fingers, curtsied. "Thank you, Alexander."

He threw me the most incendiary gaze then proceeded to empty his tray, his pert behind making the skirt of the dress sway and bounce.

My mouth went dry. I reached out to touch the white ruffle at the edge. "Oh, Vincent. My, my, my…you have been keeping secrets."

He twisted his head around to gaze at me and his blue eyes flashed mischief. "Yes, Sir."

I shook my head, clicking my tongue. "Naughty. Very naughty."

Vincent's soft lips parted, and he straightened. My gaze stroked over him from head to foot. He was a vision of loveliness. I shook my head again.

A throat cleared. I tore my attention away from Vincent and regarded Matteo, who had moved close and was now holding out a small plate of cookies toward me.

"Would you like a biscuit?" he asked.

I took my time answering while I noticed that Matteo was naked except for a snug pair of blue and black striped boxer briefs and a bowtie. Although Vincent, in his French maid get-up, was the prettier of the two, Matteo matched him in pure desirability.

"Hot," I murmured, my gaze moving up and down Matteo's body as I took a cookie from his plate and bit into it, holding his gaze as I chewed with exaggerated care, licking the crumbs from my lip.

Matteo inclined his head and took a bow. "Thank you, Sir."

He offered the plate of cookies to Alexander.

"Oh, thank you very much," Alexander said, taking one of the ginger snaps and breaking it. He popped one half into his mouth and chewed contentedly.

He certainly didn't seem uncomfortable with two men in various stages of undress. Then again, if he had been a client of Daphne's, he would have been expected to deal with a number of bizarre situations.

"Vincent," I said, staring at the polished wood floor of Daphne's living room, because I didn't dare look at him again or I might actually start drooling.

"Yes, Sir?" The delicate tones of Vincent's voice tickled my eardrums.

"I would like a cup of tea."

"Of course, Sir. Why don't you sit down?"

"That's a good idea," I said, nodding and finding a spot on the couch next to Alexander.

All of a sudden, I didn't want to be here. I didn't want to sit still and have tea and biscuits while Vincent pranced around in that outfit and teased me with an occasional flash of the ruffled white panties underneath. I almost choked on my cookie.

"Nic, are you all right?" Daphne said, giving me a strange look.

"Yes, yes, I'm fine." I waved a hand in the air, trying to convince myself that getting up and grabbing Vincent and Matteo and pulling them out the front door was an ill-advised endeavor, even though that was what I dearly wanted to do.

Instead, I made small talk with Alexander and tried not to ogle Vincent and Matteo. When Daphne returned from wherever she had been, she patted Vincent on his floofy-skirted behind as she passed, then plunked herself on the sofa between me and Alexander.

"Hey," she said, smiling at me so blithely that I was worried for her mental state.

"Hey?" I said, the corner of my mouth quirking in amusement.

"So, it turns out Alexander's into me."

"I kind of figured that out, Daphne," I said, leaning around her to finger-gun Alexander, who grinned.

"Yes, well, I..." She glanced at Alexander and giggled, then leaned in to whisper in my ear. "I'm still his Domme."

I lowered my voice. "Professionally?"

She giggled. This new, giggling Daphne was quite charming. "Oh no. Not at all."

"That's wonderful!"

She kissed me on the cheek and turned back to Alexander. "Nic and I have been friends for many, many years."

I leaned forward so I could meet Alexander's sedate gaze. "Yes, we have. So I will hear of it if you step out of line." I was sort of joking, but sort of not.

Alexander smiled, deepening the shallow grooves in the corners of his lips. "I wouldn't dare," he said, gazing with fondness at my friend, and I knew that everything would be fine...at least for now.

We finished our relaxing tea, then I asked Vincent if he would do me the favor of wearing his French maid outfit home.

"*Oui*, Monsieur. *Bien sur*," he said, acting coy, and it was all I could do to maintain some measure of control. I let Matteo get dressed, we put on our coats and I put Vincent's boots in a bag to carry. There wasn't a lot of snow left, so his cute shoes would be fine.

We took our leave and Daphne and Alexander promised to be at the art show.

Taylor had stayed at Daphne's, as he still had stuff to do and Daphne had promised to bring him back later. We had barely stepped in the door at our place when I told Vincent to hang up his jacket and stand in front of the sofa with his hands clasped behind his back. Of course, he did as he was told, sashaying in the low heels until he had positioned himself.

Matteo and I exchanged heated glances as we got out of our winter gear and joined Vincent in the living room.

Vincent grinned, looking far from the demure servant he had been at Daphne's. He knew we were completely turned on and vulnerable to his gender fluid charms, and he was taking no prisoners. He tossed his head and met my gaze dead on.

I smiled wide and inclined my chin. "Okay. If you're intent on being cheeky, my beautiful boy, let's take it to the next level."

Matteo watched me with anticipation as I licked my lips and stood in front of Vincent with my arms crossed, regarding him with purpose.

"Yes, Sir," Vincent said, the bloom in his cheeks a light, blush pink, the blue of his eyes vivid around his dilated pupils.

"Take that pretty skirt and pull it up to your chest, so I can see those divine panties I caught glimpses of earlier."

Matteo smiled as he watched Vincent take the hem of the blue skirt in his fingers and drag it upward.

"*Che bello,*" Matteo muttered as the baby-doll panties were revealed — white satin with rows of frills — that made Vincent look like he had a role at the Moulin Rouge. They were luscious and shiny and dainty in a way that delighted me, seeing them on my very pretty boy, who no doubt had an erection underneath the copious frills where it remained hidden for now.

"Matteo, would you like to give our pretty baby a blow job?"

"Indeed I would."

The skirt in Vincent's hands fluttered as he lifted it higher and gazed with longing at Matteo.

"On your knees, then. And pull down those scintillating panties so we can see what Vincent's got for us."

"Yes, Sir," Matteo said, his voice gruff as he fell to his knees before Vincent.

Vincent gasped as Matteo's fingers — probably still cold from being outside — slid beneath the delicate waistband of the baby dolls and pushed the shiny fabric down, revealing a very swollen cock that looked downright indecent beneath the blue skirt.

"Oh Lord almighty," I breathed. "I may not be a religious person, but I'm starting to think there is a God."

"Yes," Matteo sighed, his gaze on Vincent's cock as he tucked the panties under Vincent's testicles. "And I'm on my knees before him."

"You can do whatever you want with that cock, Matteo, but it had better include your mouth and maybe your hands…and an epic orgasm. Or two, if you want to jerk yourself off."

Matteo closed his eyes and sighed. "Yes, Sir."

I settled down to watch as Matteo got busy. The reverence with which he carried out his task was admirable and a joy to watch.

But I couldn't tear my eyes away from Vincent, who stood there like a vision, his skirt pulled up, arms akimbo, delicate fingers clutching the hem of his skirt, mouth open and eyes closed, head back, as Matteo attended to him.

The tableau they made was almost too much. In fact…

"I'm getting my phone. I need to record this," I said, but I don't think either of them heard me.

I went to scoop my phone out of my jacket pocket and returned to the living room. Vincent looked even more wanton, as Matteo held the base of Vincent's erection in one hand and used his mouth on Vincent's length in a frenzied, lust-driven assault. Vincent had let go of the skirt with his left hand and now braced it against Matteo's shoulder. Matteo was jerking his own cock dry, although he took a moment to spit into his palm before returning to Vincent.

The sounds of harsh breaths, small grunts and long moans filled the otherwise-quiet space.

There was no point asking for their consent to video the proceedings, because that would pull them right out of it. I felt a little bad going ahead, but they honestly needed to see this after it was all over. I'd let them dictate what was done with the footage, whether it would be deleted or saved to our secure hard drive, where we had quite a scintillating collection of performances. I did try to make a habit of gaining consent beforehand, but this had taken us all by surprise.

"I'm coming… I'm coming," Vincent said, then cried out as he clutched Matteo and stared at his own dick erupting over Matteo's tongue as Matteo swallowed him down.

"Jesus fucking Christ," I breathed. The blue satin and white ruffles, the black stockings and shoes, the garters, Vincent's androgynous beauty and Matteo's blatant hunger, combined to make this one of the most arousing things I'd witnessed in a long time, even though I lived with these men on a daily, domestic basis.

While I watched and recorded, Matteo made a strangled sound around Vincent's dick as his own cock erupted over his knuckles and white jizz streamed down his fist to his muscled forearm.

* * * *

Later, upstairs, after Matteo and I took turns sucking him to fullness again, Vincent fucked me while wearing the baby blue maid's outfit, and Matteo lifted his skirt and entered him from behind, pounding him so hard it was as if Matteo were fucking me with Vincent's dick. I think I had about three or four orgasms before Vincent came and Matteo soon after. We ended up a sweaty, satisfied mess.

"I'm going to have to thank Daphne for ordering you that outfit," I said, when I could speak again. Vincent lay face down on the bed, completely spent and satisfied, not moving or opening his eyes. But he smiled as I moved a stray bit of hair off his sweaty forehead and snuggled into the pillow. Matteo cleaned up and joined us and we drifted off, full of tea and tiny sandwiches and a communal sense of achievement.

Chapter Five

Matteo was in a good mood.

He'd completed a couple of long-standing projects at work and was plating his famous sole with white wine sauce while joking with Vincent. Because he was, in general, a serious fellow, when Matteo felt jaunty and relaxed, it was noticeable. It didn't happen that often, but when it did, his lightened mood spread betwixt the rest of us.

By the time we sat down to eat, he was practically effervescent, and there was a brightness to his eyes that we needed to see more of.

"Cheer up, Matteo," I teased.

He shook his head. "I don't know why I'm so giddy. It was nice to see Daphne yesterday. I'm glad life is treating her well." He threw a bashful glance at Vincent. "And I did so enjoy our little, ahem, *tête-a-tête*, when we got home."

Taylor put his hands over his ears.

"Yes, I agree about Daphne," I said. "This thing with Alexander was a surprise, but I wish her all the best. He seems like a decent guy."

Taylor lowered his hands and went back to eating. "She's killing it with her OnlyFans. She's making some decent side money now," Taylor said, slurping up his fish. "Fuck, this is delicious."

"Manners," I said. "You don't need to swear at the table."

"Shit, sorry. Oh damn. Whatever. Anyway, it's *delicioso*."

"*Grazie*," Matteo murmured, just before a song started playing from his phone, which lay on the counter.

I glanced at the phone, then at Matteo, not paying much attention. But Matteo had stiffened and paled as he stared at the chiming phone and now began to stand.

He seemed to realize what he was doing and hastened to apologize, folding his napkin and leaving it on his chair.

"I'm sorry. Excuse me, but I have to get this."

"Okay," I said, glancing at Vincent, who seemed as surprised as I was. We had a policy of no phones at the table, which Matteo had never had a problem with before. I tried to remember if I'd ever heard his phone ring prior to this. I'd never heard his phone play *Landslide* by Fleetwood Mac.

In a moment he had picked it up and swiped his thumb across the screen, holding it to his ear.

"Zarah? Is that you?"

His voice shook as he asked the question then he smiled so wide I thought his face would split open. "Oh God!"

He seemed to remember we were there, but only glanced at me and held up a finger as he hastened from the room.

I looked at Vincent and Taylor. Everyone was poised with their utensils in the air, wondering what on earth was happening. For Matteo to get up and answer his phone in the middle of the fancy meal he'd cooked was unprecedented.

Who the fuck is Zarah?

"Has Matteo ever mentioned anyone named Zarah to you?" I asked Vincent.

He shook his head. I turned to Taylor.

"You?"

"Nope." Taylor shrugged and went back to eating.

I tried, but was unable to resume, and Vincent seemed to be in the same predicament.

After several moments, Matteo came back into the dining room. He held his phone to his chest and gazed at us with shining eyes out of a flushed face.

"That was… That was my daughter Zarah on the phone," he said.

And my world shifted.

"Your…daughter?" I echoed.

Matteo inhaled a breath, almost as if he was choking. "Yes."

I glanced at Vincent, who seemed as gobsmacked as I was. "Why didn't we know you had a daughter?"

"I'm sorry. I'm so sorry. I never told you."

"No," Vincent murmured. "You never did. I don't—"

"I never mentioned her because I've had to live as if she never existed."

"I don't—I don't understand," I said.

"She told me to stay away from her and her husband. But I've just found out she's been manipulated and controlled by this — this *horrible* man for years, and she's finally left him."

He blinked back tears, but one escaped and trickled over his cheek. "She wants to meet with me," he said in a voice filled with emotion.

Holy shit. Before I could get to him, Vincent stood and stepped forward, wrapping Matteo in his arms.

"Oh my God, Matteo," Vincent said.

Taylor and I followed suit, recognizing a man brought to a place he'd given up on ever seeing again.

"I wish you hadn't kept such an important part of you a secret," I murmured.

"I'm so sorry, Nic. It was easier if I just pretended I didn't have a — a daughter," Matteo whispered.

"We're going to have to talk about this," I murmured, but I tightened my hold on Matteo.

"I know," he said. "I'm so sorry."

"We'll figure it out," I affirmed.

Matteo nodded and pulled back from us. "I told her about you two, who you are to me, about our arrangement. She said she wants to meet you both. Maybe tomorrow?"

I nodded, looking at Vincent and Taylor. "Sure."

"Okay, good. Thank you."

We didn't say anything more about it. We hadn't met Zarah yet, and it seemed too early to dissect this new development.

* * * *

Matteo arranged for Zarah to come by after supper the next day. He hadn't really explained the situation any more than to say he was sorry to have kept her a secret from all of us. After the first couple of times, I told him to leave it alone, that we'd talk about it in depth at a later date. Zarah was his daughter, and we looked forward to meeting her. The fact that she knew who we were to her father and still wanted to meet us was reassuring, even if this entire situation was unnerving and unexpected.

Zarah had deep brown hair and eyes, like Matteo, but her complexion was much darker than his, indicating the influence of an additional ethnicity. She was stunning, with bold intelligent eyes, an assertive nose and a lush mouth—standing as tall as Matteo.

"Zarah, these are Nic and Vincent, my partners," Matteo said.

"I'm so pleased to meet you!" Zarah said with sincerity.

"Welcome, Zarah," I said, holding out a hand that she shook with eagerness.

"Hi," Vincent said, shaking her hand after I did, a cautious look on his face.

"And this is Taylor," Matteo said, "our son."

Taylor stepped forward. He cleared his throat and threw me a glance before offering Zarah a smile. "Hey, sis."

I wanted to kiss Matteo for being bold enough to reinforce Taylor's validity in this household.

Zarah frowned. She looked back and forth between Matteo and Taylor. "I don't understand. I'm sorry. Your...son?"

Taylor laughed, his contagious amusement lightening the mood in the room.

"Well, not by blood...but by circumstance?" He glanced at Matteo, who nodded.

Zarah's face indicated understanding. "Oh. I see."

"Welcome to the family," Taylor said, expressing what Vincent and I had not.

Taylor's maturity shocked us out of our reticence.

"Yes, welcome, Zarah. It's very nice to…meet you," I managed.

Vincent smiled and said, "Yes. We didn't know Matteo had a daughter." He shot an accusing glance Matteo's way, and Zarah flushed.

"Zarah, I'm so sorry," Matteo said. "I…it was just easier to pretend—"

"I know, Dad. It's not your fault."

"It's not your fault, either," Matteo said with conviction.

Zarah rolled her eyes and sighed. "Yes, it is. I'm the one that married a horrible"—her breath caught in her throat—"*horrible* person."

She started to cry, and Matteo sat her on the sofa, gathering her head to his chest, letting her sob into his shoulder and shooting a helpless glance my way.

"Vincent, let's go make a pot of tea," I said, taking his sleeve in my fingers and pulling him out of the room. Taylor followed us to the kitchen.

I got the teapot down without a word and took the kettle to the sink, filling it silently as I tried to catch up to everything that had happened. Vincent got the teacups and the sugar and milk.

"I mean, what Matteo said makes sense—that he was pretending she didn't exist because he wasn't allowed to see her," Taylor continued.

I nodded. "It makes perfect sense."

"But you're still mad."

"Taylor, I'm not mad. I'm just…fucking stunned, and I honestly do feel a bit betrayed."

"Which is understandable," Vincent said, glancing my way. "Me, too."

"But you heard what they said. It sounds like her husband is an abusive, controlling freakshow."

"Yes."

I stared at the floor, thinking, my brain spinning.

"What?" Vincent asked.

"Not to be alarmist, but it's usually when a person decides to leave the relationship that an already-abusive partner becomes violent."

Vincent and Taylor exchanged a glance.

"I'll find out where she's staying. I can't offer her a room here." I glanced at Taylor. "We're kind of full."

"I mean, I can go stay with Riley..."

"No," I said, giving him a look that said I meant business. "I'm sure Zarah is in a safe situation for the moment, otherwise Matteo would have said something."

Matteo poked his head into the kitchen. He was wearing his coat.

"Nic, Vincent, I'm taking Zarah for coffee. There's a lot that we need to talk about." He smiled apologetically.

"I'm sure," I said, returning his smile. "Of course."

"Thanks. I shouldn't be too late."

"Take your time. It sounds like you two haven't been able to talk for a while," Vincent said. "It'll be good to catch up."

Matteo's eyes shone as he nodded to Vincent. "Thank you." He turned to leave the room, then hesitated. "I'm so sorry. I didn't mean to mislead you."

I shrugged. "Got any other children you need to tell us about? Or ex-wives or murderous in-laws?"

Matteo licked his lips, absorbing my question and perhaps realizing it was a fair one, under the circumstances. "Zarah's mother died when she was in her late teens."

"I'm sorry, Matteo. You could have mentioned her."

"I know."

* * * *

As I lay beside Vincent, trying to get to sleep, I listened to the silence of the house and Vincent's deep breathing, waiting for sounds of the front door opening upon Matteo's return. It was almost midnight. They'd gone for coffee at six o'clock.

Before he'd gone to sleep, Vincent had suggested they'd probably got talking and lost track of time. When you hadn't seen your child for years, I supposed there would be a fair bit to catch up on.

Still, an uneasy feeling had settled in my gut, which could have been residual tension from everything that had happened over the past two days. I wondered if parents of teenagers felt this way when their kids were out late, and I realized how responsible Taylor was in this regard. We always knew where he was and when he'd be home, and he'd update us by text or phone call if there was any change to his plans. But Matteo was a grown man who made sensible decisions, so I wasn't worried about his safety—only that the sense of discombobulation I'd experienced upon finding out that Matteo had kept Zarah a secret from us made me less sure of how things stood. It was as if I'd discovered a crack in my favorite pot and wondered if it could still be relied upon.

It was unsettling, to say the least. Those initial feelings of betrayal had subsided because his reasoning made a lot of sense, especially when I considered how sensitive and emotional Matteo could be under his stoic surface. But I still felt the instability of finding out everything was not as it had seemed. I hoped that once Matteo, Vincent and I spoke more about Zarah and what her appearance in Matteo's life meant to our relationship, those feelings would go away.

I must have drifted off. When I woke in the darkness to the gentle sounds of Vincent's breathing and no third body in the bed with me, I looked at the clock. It was one-thirty.

I wondered if Matteo had come home but not come to bed. I slipped out from beside Vincent and grabbed the long sweater I used as a robe, wrapping it around myself and pulling on a pair of wool socks against the cold floors.

There was a light on in the living room, but it wasn't Matteo. Rather, it was Taylor, playing a video game.

"He's home, Nic. Don't worry," Taylor said with a wry smile.

I snorted a half-hearted laugh. "I'm not worried."

"Yeah, okay. He just came in. Try the bathroom."

"Oh." I yawned, relief flooding me. "Good idea."

I returned to the hall and sure enough, saw light escaping from behind the cracked-open door. I knocked as I registered the sound of running water.

"Hey, you're back," I said.

"Yeah," Matteo answered. "Sorry I'm so late."

"It's okay," I said, nudging the door open enough that I could see him.

He didn't look up from where he was washing his hands at the sink, staring at the water with his brows furrowed.

"You're bleeding," I said, looking at the pink water going down the drain. "Tell me you didn't punch Zarah," I said, humor my only recourse in the situation. A chill went down my spine as Matteo regarded me skeptically.

"Of course I didn't punch Zarah," he said, clearing his throat. "I fell. On the pavement. There's fucking ice everywhere."

I blinked, because Matteo didn't swear often. But what he had said about the ice was true.

"Are you okay?"

"I'm fine. You don't have to worry about me."

"That ship has sailed, Matteo. I do worry about you."

I stared at the shredded knuckles of his right hand. It didn't add up. If he'd fallen, shouldn't the palms of his hands be bleeding?

But it was late, and I was glad he was home. We could talk about it in the morning.

He turned off the tap and took the hand towel I offered, patting his knuckles with it carefully.

"Do you need a Band-Aid?"

"No. It's fine."

I nodded, backing out so he could exit the bathroom. "Coming to bed?"

"In a minute. I'm going to hang out with Taylor. I'm too wired to sleep."

"Okay. Sure." I leaned in to kiss him on the cheek. "Don't be long."

"I won't," he said, turning to kiss me back.

As I walked upstairs, I wondered why he had lied about his hand and who had been on the receiving end of the punch, or punches, he had thrown. I felt like I knew the answer to that question, but I didn't want to examine it right now. He was home, he was safe and he was ours, and that was all that mattered.

A little later, Matteo came into the room, undressed and slipped into bed beside Vincent. It was only at that point I was able to relax enough to fall back asleep, putting the other stuff out of my mind for now.

* * * *

My alarm woke me at six-fifteen. I shut it off and turned to see that Matteo and Vincent were already gone, presumably downstairs getting breakfast, since I couldn't hear the shower running. The tumultuous events of the previous day came back to me. I pushed off the covers and headed into the bathroom for a perfunctory shower. I had a full day of classes and needed to talk to Matteo before he left for work.

Vincent was tidying up from breakfast when I got downstairs, although he handed me a coffee and a plate of cold toast.

"Good morning. I thought you'd be down earlier," he said as I gave him a kiss on the cheek.

"Thanks. I didn't sleep well. Must have hit the snooze on my alarm. I don't remember doing it but…"

Matteo came in the room, holding his cell to his ear, speaking in hushed tones. He grabbed a pen and paper and went into the other room.

Fuck it. I exchanged a glance with Vincent, who shrugged. "He's been on the phone most of the morning."

"Yeah?"

"I think it's Zarah. It must be."

"Which is understandable, I suppose. They've been apart a long time," I said.

"Yes," he echoed.

I ate a couple of bites of the cold toast, realized I had no appetite and threw it back on the plate. I sipped my coffee, staring at the table.

"Are you all right, Nic?"

"I'm fine. Just...worried."

"That's not like you."

"I think Matteo punched someone's face last night. He came home with blood on his knuckles."

Vincent's mouth opened, then closed. "Holy shit," he said after a few seconds.

"Yeah. And also, it's the disruption of" — I waved my hand in the direction of Matteo — "everything."

"Our usual morning routine?"

"I suppose. Yes. It's a comfort, you know? It's something I can predict. Zarah has, unfortunately, taken my predictable life and smashed it, at least for the moment."

Vincent nodded. "I think we need to get together for a scene or something."

I shook my head. "Matteo's too distracted."

"Wouldn't that help take his mind off everything?"

"I don't know if he wants to do that. He must be thrilled to have Zarah back in his life."

"I thought so, originally. But he's seemed so stressed out. We should talk to him," Vincent suggested.

I nodded, and when Matteo poked his head in to give us a vague wave goodbye before he headed off to work, I lifted my chin.

"Hold up. We need to talk to you."

Matteo seemed startled. "But I'll be late for work."

I narrowed my eyes. Matteo didn't normally act like this. His job was his job. It didn't interfere with our lives, and it always took a back seat to more urgent things.

"You'll be fine." I pulled out a chair. "Sit."

He looked like he wanted to argue with me but he sat.

"I'm sorry," he said.

"For what?"

"For whatever you're mad about."

"Matteo, I'm not mad. But I need to know whose face got the attention of your knuckles last night."

Matteo paled and moved his hand farther under the table. "I fell."

"Try again."

"I scraped my knuckles on the pavement. Really, I — "

I slapped the surface of the table with my palm, and hell it felt good. It made a really satisfying sound, too, making both Matteo and Vincent jerk.

"Don't *lie* to me. Don't start outright lying to me, Matteo. A lie of omission is one thing, but when you look me in the eyes and tell me something that's not true, I draw the line. I won't accept it. Tell me where you were last night and why your knuckles were bleeding. I'm not a fucking idiot."

Matteo's lips pursed together as if he were waging an internal war.

"Is Zarah asking you to lie?"

"No! She's — She's the victim here!"

"Of who? Her ex?"

Matteo nodded. "He threatened her. What the hell was I supposed to do?"

I blinked. "Oh, I don't know, maybe go to the police?"

"She's *gone* to the police!" he stated, staring me down. "They've done nothing, Nic. *Nothing!*"

I gazed at Matteo, who had never shouted at me before this moment. My voice was quiet when I said, "Did you punch him? Zarah's husband?"

Matteo suddenly looked like he might cry. He pushed a breath through his lips and said, "Yes."

"Just one punch?"

Matteo shrugged.

"Oh my God, Matteo." I put a shaking hand to my forehead. I didn't give a damn about Zarah's husband, but I didn't want Matteo to get into trouble.

"Zarah's pregnant," he said.

Chapter Six

"What? Jesus." I took that in. "Is it his?"

Matteo looked at me like I was from another planet. "Yes."

I held up my hand to apologize in silence for the question.

Vincent watched the exchange, his face appearing paler by the second. He chewed his lip.

"Is she…don't get mad, but…is she going to keep it?" I asked, my eyes down, my voice hushed.

Matteo sighed. "She doesn't know yet."

I nodded, then sat down, not sure what to say. Matteo took the seat next to me.

"I thought you were going to be late," I said.

"I don't care anymore," Matteo replied.

I nodded again. "Well, what the fuck are we going to do, Matteo?"

"This has nothing to do with you and Vincent. It's *my* mess."

I couldn't contain my outrage. I glared at Matteo. "It's *our* mess! We are partners—you and Vincent and me. We are a family. And Zarah's part of this family. This affects all of us."

"But you shouldn't have to deal with *any* of this."

I shifted in my seat, the anger receding as quickly as it had gathered. I stared at the table, then my eyes landed on Matteo's beat-up knuckles. The blood had scabbed and the cuts didn't look too bad.

Still...

I reached out and took his hand, smoothing my thumb over the unbroken skin near the cuts. "You could have been hurt," I said, my voice shaky. "He could have had a gun. Matteo. I—"

He squeezed my fingers. "I know. I'm sorry."

Vincent wrapped his hand around ours, careful not to touch the sore spots on Matteo's knuckles.

"What if he presses charges?" I said, the fear sitting like a lump in my stomach. "Did he defend himself?"

The corner of Matteo's mouth quirked but then he sobered. "He tried."

"Oh fuck. You didn't maim him, did you?" I was pretty sure Matteo would never be that cruel, even to a lowlife who had mistreated his daughter. Then again, I'd assumed Matteo had no family of his own before us, and I'd been wrong about that.

"No, Nic, I'm not an animal. I just wanted him to know what would happen if he ever came near Zarah again...or the baby, which he doesn't even know about and hopefully won't find out about." He squeezed my hand, hard. "Thank you. And I'm sorry."

"Never mind. Where is Zarah now? Is she somewhere safe?"

"Yes. She's at a friend's place. A friend who owns a rotty and a pit bull."

"Oh. That's good." I glanced at Vincent. "Maybe *we* should get a pit bull."

He smiled, knowing I was bullshitting. "Taylor would be thrilled, except we don't need one. We have Matteo."

Matteo blushed and rolled his eyes, but I smiled, and it was a relief to have some humor applied to the situation.

"You said Zarah's mother passed away?" I said, addressing the elephant in the room.

"She died a long time ago. We'd already split up. I was moderately involved in Zarah's life at that point, although her mother had issues with my...pastimes. I'd tried to keep them secret, but it was difficult. I'm not ashamed of my tastes or of anything about my sexuality."

I squeezed his hand again, giving him a nod.

"Look... Please don't go anywhere near this guy again, Matteo. Not alone. If there's a problem, tell us, and we'll all go, or we'll go to the police. But I won't have you putting yourself in danger in such a reckless way again."

"Okay."

I cleared my throat, meeting his gaze with my Dom look.

He nodded once. "Yes, Sir."

We were silent for a few beats.

"May I go to work now, Sir?" Matteo asked in a hushed voice.

I released him with some reluctance. "You may. But please come straight home when you're done. We need you here tonight."

"Yes, Sir."

* * * *

That evening, after we'd had supper and Matteo had touched base with Zarah to make sure she was okay and that her husband hadn't tried to contact her, I took him and Vincent upstairs.

Taylor had gone to Daphne's because one of her regular clients had requested an appearance from Sparky. Some of her clients remembered the young man dressed in tight shorts and a leather pup hood who had passed Daphne the instruments she used to debase them. Taylor got a kick out of it and now occasionally revisited his role when requested. He was beginning to learn the basics of shibari rope work from Daphne in his role as helper.

We had the house to ourselves. The events of the previous day had shaken the foundations of our relationship, and we needed to reconnect and confirm that we were still a united partnership.

Matteo looked nervous and reluctant as Vincent and I started to remove our clothes.

"What's wrong?" I asked him.

"I feel like I've betrayed you both. I'm so sorry." He took a sudden inhale that broke on a half-sob. "I'm sorry I didn't tell you about this part of my…life."

I glanced at Vincent, who was now in nothing but a sweet pair of lacy purple panties with ruffled edges. I was down to boxer briefs, a sports bra and an open white button-down. We moved toward Matteo at the same time.

"I'm sorry, too," I said, gazing into Matteo's eyes with conviction. "We want you to share everything with us. We thought you had." I pulled him into my arms.

Matteo's face crumpled as he returned my embrace. Vincent put his long arms around us both, and we huddled together until Matteo stopped shaking.

"Your problems are our problems," Vincent whispered, nuzzling Matteo's stubbled cheek.

"Thank you," Matteo replied in a quiet voice. "I'm so sorry."

I snorted and detached myself from the embrace.

"Okay, now. That's enough apologizing." I pointed at him. "Get naked — unless you're too emotional to have some fun with us?" I asked, gazing at him with my eyebrows raised.

He shook his head. "No. I think…I'll take off my clothes, Sir."

"Excellent," I said, clapping my hands together and licking my lips. "Nothing too strenuous, but I want to make sure both of you know you can bring any problem to me, no matter how big" — I glanced at Vincent's erection — "or small it might be. Vincent, you don't have any secrets, do you?"

Vincent gave me an innocent and angelic look. "Nothing that you haven't *rooted* out of me by now. Sir."

"Touché," I said, moving close and wrapping my arms around his waist, peering at the ruffled panties and making a clicking noise with my tongue. "Those panties are ridiculously cute. I love them."

"So do I," Matteo said. "Very, very much."

"Vincent, lie down on your back. I want Matteo to show us just how much he likes those pretty panties."

"Yes, of course, Sir," Vincent said, arranging himself the way I'd told him to. He spread himself wide, long arms and legs reaching for the corners of the bed, his hooded gaze on Matteo.

Matteo regarded Vincent like a connoisseur of all things delicate and masculine. He slowly removed his clothes, shooting the occasional glance my way as I leaned against the dresser and watched, my arms folded. The best part of having two partners was the ability to indulge one's voyeuristic urges. My men loved to perform for me, and I so loved to watch them with each other, especially when my position as Dom allowed me to orchestrate and maneuver them according to my wishes.

"Get to it, Matteo. I want you to kiss that cheeky boy over those ridiculous panties until he's begging you to rip them off him."

Matteo nodded. We exchanged a significant gaze. I think we were both glad to get back to something familiar and enjoyable that reestablished our connection.

He turned to Vincent and crawled with care overtop of the spread-eagled boy on the blue sheets. Vincent lifted his chin as if in challenge as he regarded Matteo's predatory stance, widening his legs and fisting his hands. He knew he was about to be tortured past the point of decency.

Matteo placed his hands on either side of Vincent's narrow hips, bracing himself above the delectable tableau. Their gazes met, and Vincent let a wash of air out between his lips.

Matteo's gaze shifted to Vincent's cock, which was thickening under the purple lace. He bent to place a chaste kiss against it, then began dotting similar kisses all along its increasing length and below, to Vincent's testicles.

"Oh," Vincent murmured, his gaze fixed on the top of Matteo's head, as Matteo took his time, worshipping Vincent as I'd commanded.

Soft sounds of pleasure from both men suffused the room as Matteo took his sweet time, laving Vincent over the lace, teasing him with persistence and delicacy until the panties were soaked with his saliva and Vincent's pre-ejaculate. By that time, Vincent was struggling to stay still as Matteo continued his attentive seduction. Vincent clenched and unclenched his hands as they lay beside where Matteo was kissing and licking him. It was all he could do to leave Matteo alone.

"Vincent, go ahead and touch Matteo. But don't change your position," I said in a hushed voice to keep them in their intimate moment.

Immediately, Vincent's hands unclenched, and he threaded his fingers into Matteo's thick hair as Vincent pulled Matteo's face down onto him. He rutted against the teasing pressure of Matteo's soft kisses until I had to warn him.

"Uh-uh. Stop that," I said. "Lie still."

Vincent gave an irritated grunt but stopped lifting himself up to meet Matteo's mouth. He continued to twine his fingers in Matteo's hair as he stuttered pleas for mercy.

I let him suffer for a little while. Then I told Matteo to take Vincent's panties down and suck him properly.

"Yes, Sir," Matteo replied, getting right to it.

Matteo's hard cock bobbed as he moved to obey my instructions. He slid his fingers under the waistband and pulled the purple lace down over Vincent's straining cock.

"Oh fuck, oh fuck," Vincent panted, gazing down at Matteo with dark eyes. "Matteo."

"Vincent, my love," Matteo said before wrapping his lips around the head of Vincent's dick.

"Ah! Oh!" Vincent gasped, rocking his hips as Matteo took him inside. "Fuuuuck. Shiiit."

I smiled. My sweet boy didn't use such language very often, but he was clearly quite overcome.

My gaze met his and a surge of arousal tore through me. We were connected, Vincent and I, perhaps more viscerally than Matteo and him or Matteo and me. It didn't mean we loved Matteo any less, only that Vincent and I had always had an immediate and powerful symbiotic connection that made itself known in erotic encounters. We were almost two sides of the same person. And Matteo was the partner we both needed.

Matteo held Vincent's hips down with his strong hands and used his throat and mouth to bring him close to orgasm. The sounds Vincent was making indicated he was about to go off.

"Stop, Matteo. Pull up," I said, watching avidly as Matteo slid his mouth off Vincent's dick and the shiny appendage swayed and twitched in the cold air.

"Sir! Nic!" Vincent groaned, trying to thrust but unable to since Matteo kept a firm hold. He made a frustrated sound and slammed his fist against the mattress.

"What's the matter, Vincent? Did you think Matteo was going to make you come?"

"Yes. Yes!"

"Oh. What a shame then. Maybe soon."

Vincent whimpered.

"And maybe not."

For an hour I had Matteo suck and lick Vincent to the point right before orgasm, then stop before Vincent tipped over the edge. In the past, this game had sometimes resulted in a pre-emptive result, because Vincent was so responsive, and I didn't always stop Matteo in time. But today, Vincent performed admirably as he was brought to the brink and back so many times.

By the time an hour was up, they were a sweaty, exhausted mess, quivering with unspent desire and likely frustrated beyond measure. I had just told Matteo to stop, yet again, and Vincent let out a desperate wail as his dick swayed helplessly over his belly and Matteo panted above him.

"No. No. Please…" Vincent whimpered. "Please."

I moved close and peered down at his flushed face. "Do you think you've been a good boy?"

"Yes. Oh yes."

"Do you think you deserve an orgasm?"

"Yes. Please, yes. Please, Sir."

"Matteo?"

"Yes, Sir?"

"Do you think Vincent should be allowed to come this time?"

Matteo peered down at Vincent's taut form and smiled.

"I suppose we could allow it. If you think so, Sir."

"Hmm. Sure. Why not? But I'm going to make him ask you nicely."

"Matteo, make me come. Please, make me come. Please, please, *please*."

Matteo and I exchanged an amused gaze before Matteo bent to his work.

Vincent clutched Matteo's head as his lips parted on a gasp. Matteo ramped up his throat work and brought Vincent close again.

"You going to come, Vincent?" I asked.

"Yes. Yes! Oh. Fuck! Fuck. Ah!" Vincent choked on more curses as he emptied into Matteo's mouth, holding Matteo down to take it all. Matteo swallowed everything and circled Vincent's hips with his powerful forearms, consuming his pleasure like a benign incubus.

* * * *

The play party we'd RSVP'd to was on Friday and provided a much-needed escape after all the heavy shit we'd gone through.

I had decided to completely Dom out for this, and bring Vincent and Matteo as my official subs. It made sense, since that was the dynamic we enjoyed, but we could have attended as an informal polyamorous unit and participated — or not — as we wished. Even in a more formal representation, there was always room for flexibility at these events — or, at least, at the events I'd attended. I liked the trappings of the lifestyle sometimes, but I had no interest in rigid roles or uncompromising traditions. To me, the heart of a kink lifestyle existed in the souls and emotions of the practitioners, not in the physical trappings, titles or rituals.

The parties I chose to attend were safe places for queer people to explore identities and fetishes in a positive way. As long as everyone treated each other with respect and a lack of preconceptions, the evening would be a success.

This particular party, called *Blast the Heat, a Midwinter Fetish Celebration*, was being hosted by a prestigious queer kink club, which had a great reputation for safe, respectful and well-organized events. They had rented the basement and first floor of a heritage building that used to serve as a church. I had to admit, the thought of kinking it up in a former church did tickle my irony-bone in a very good way. To me and to many people in the lifestyle, kink served as a sensual form of worship and a vehicle for transcendence. The location wasn't as incongruous as it seemed, even though most religious people would have an issue with my reasoning.

After getting dressed, I waited downstairs for Matteo and Vincent, drinking some water as I doubted I'd want to have the bother of enjoying refreshments at the event. We were attending for the kink, not the food. I'd selected a pair of snug black leather pants, with a dark plum button-down, untucked. Overtop, I wore a velvet blazer in a lighter purple shade, that I'd ordered online a few weeks earlier. Not the traditional Dom trappings, necessarily, but I felt they gave me the stature I needed and the class I wanted. I felt attractive, my dysphoria hovering in the background while I got ready. Once we were on our way, it would disappear entirely.

Matteo came down shortly after I did, dressed in the outfit Vincent and I had chosen for him.

"Hello, you naughty little boy. You're late for school," I said with a salacious smile.

Matteo grinned and blushed, then bowed to me when he reached the bottom of the stairs. "So sorry, Sir."

He wore a pair of navy, knee-length cotton shorts with pleats at the waist, held up with suspenders over a short-sleeved white button-down. A classic black bowtie, white ankle socks and black loafers finished off the outfit.

"Wait a second," I said, remembering the Blue Jays cap Daphne had given me for my birthday as a joke. I dug it out of a bin in the hall and placed it onto Matteo's head. "Now, you're ready."

"Thank you, Sir."

The baseball cap gave Matteo an even more boyish appearance and added a sense of cheeky fun. Matteo seemed to get a kick out of it, being on the verge of turning forty.

"I need a lollipop or something."

I laughed. "Oh, I'll give you a lollipop, don't worry. But we need to get to the club first. And we're still waiting for—"

"Me." Vincent's voice came from above us.

We looked up, and Matteo took a sharp inhale of breath, then breathed out, "*Che bello*, Vincent. *Bellissimo!*"

All I could do was smile.

Vincent wore a pair of gold pants that fit like skinny jeans but glittered and outlined every curve and line of his sleekly muscled thighs and calves. The pants had detailing to suggest knee pads, and zippers at the ankle, to give them a motorcycle look. He'd paired them with his purple Docs, which he'd polished to a high gleam, and a snug black shirt with three-quarter length sleeves, that skimmed the waistband of the jeans, giving glimpses of pale skin whenever he moved or reached to touch his hair. Around his neck he wore a pretty velvet choker with a single, sizeable pearl hanging from the center.

He looked beautiful and fuckable and ethereal.

He'd enhanced his eyes with a deep plum liner that brought out the blue in his irises. His hair, growing out from its short, spiked cut, looked like a pixie shag now, and he'd defined the jagged edges with glittered gel.

"Oh baby. *Slay*," I breathed out.

Vincent posed.

Matteo swallowed, his Adam's apple bobbing, and stepped forward, holding out his hand to the vision descending the stairs. Vincent rested his hand in Matteo's and Matteo wrapped his fingers around Vincent's, leading him down the steps.

"You're a vision," Matteo whispered, leaning toward Vincent.

Vincent wrapped a hand around Matteo's neck, pulling him in for an open-mouthed kiss.

I crossed my arms and watched them together. After a moment, they pulled apart and gazed at me with serene satisfaction.

"Oh, don't mind me. I'm enjoying the show."

Matteo stroked Vincent's hair, and I could tell he'd be happy to stay here and play for the rest of the evening, but we had a party to get to.

"Shouldn't we be going?" Vincent said, his cheeks rosy with excitement.

"Indeed." I grinned, putting my hands in my pockets. "I can't wait to show you both off. I shall be the envy of everyone. So…rules for the evening."

They gave me their rapt attention, and, for about the thousandth time, I wondered how I'd gotten so lucky.

"I'm not going to let you out of my sight. We will decide as a group and individually if we want to play. I'm not letting anyone touch either of you in an intimate way, unless you give express permission beforehand. Got it?"

"Yes, Sir."
"Perfect. Then let's go."

Chapter Seven

We arrived about thirty minutes after the official start time, even though I had planned on being punctual. I hated being late, even when it was fashionable. But tonight, nothing would ruin my mood. I had a stunning man on each arm and felt like I ruled the world.

I took Vincent's gloved hand and brought him forward. He wore his calf-length, black wool coat over his gold skinny jeans and black T, with a fuzzy, hot pink scarf wrapped around his neck and an ivory knitted hat with a huge purple pom-pom that I tweaked every once in a while, to his amusement.

I had on my best leather coat that hit mid-thigh and made me look taller somehow, with a gray plaid scarf and no hat, and Matteo wore his navy pea coat, which looked perfect over his schoolboy uniform. The Blue Jays hat added that little bit of extra to his outfit and also kept the heat in, although it wasn't designed for winter. I don't think Matteo had ever worn a baseball cap in his life, which made it an extra-amusing accessory.

We descended two sets of stone stairs, into a spacious vestibule that amplified the gentle strains of a string ensemble and the hum of conversation from the main part of the basement.

Two young people — one beefy and blond, the other slight with shoulder-length black hair — in leather collars and snug black rubber shirts sat, smiling at us in an amenable manner.

"Hi there. Are you on the list for *Blast the Heat*?" the beefy tow-headed man asked.

"Yes, we are. Nic Walker, Vincent Blake and Matteo Rossi."

He scanned the list of names in front of him. "Ah, yes. Here you are."

He checked off our names while the other person stamped our hands and gestured for us to go through. "Off you go, then. Have fun!" they said, their gazes lingering on Matteo and Vincent.

"Oh, we intend to," I said, giving him a salute.

A young woman in a rubber body suit, also wearing a leather collar, stepped forward.

"Welcome to *Blast the Heat*. May I take your coats?"

"Yes, thank you," I replied.

We let her look after our outerwear. Vincent brushed invisible dust off his glittery pants as a flush suffused his cheeks. His hands opened and closed with excess energy.

I gave him a kiss on the cheek to reassure him. "You. Look. Stunning." I smiled, happy when he returned it. "Come on. Let's own this party."

He laughed and nodded. "Yes."

I moved forward, my subs keeping step behind me. They caused heads to turn and gentle exclamations of astonishment. And if eyes had been hands, they would have needed a complete disinfect after crossing the room.

"Welcome to *Blast the Heat!*" said a man in diminutive silver shorts as he offered us drinks from a tray. "Would you care for some sparkling lemonade?"

"Thank you," I replied with a nod, taking a glass. The server inclined his head and moved on. I turned to Matteo. "Here. Drink."

Matteo's eyes flashed with desire as I tipped the glass to his lips so that he could take a sip. Vincent watched with clear interest as a drop of lemonade escaped the glass and dripped down Matteo's clean-shaven chin.

"Vincent, get that, will you? Use your tongue," I suggested.

Vincent ducked his head and licked the drop of lemonade from Matteo's chin. The sight was as erotic as if Vincent had gone to his knees to lick Matteo's cock. Maybe more so.

"Now, why don't you give Matteo a kiss on his wet lips."

Vincent smiled and his ethereal beauty took my breath away. "Of course, Sir," he said, cupping Matteo's chin and leaning in to kiss him with a lackadaisical air that made me hard.

"Well, fuck," I said, my smile wide. "Shall we go see what kind of *heat blasting* is on offer this evening?"

"Definitely," Vincent said as I drained my glass, placing it onto a nearby server's tray, and moved forward into the dim space.

The cavernous basement of the heritage building offered a place for people to mingle, converse and listen to the quartet of musicians who were ensconced in the corner. Along two walls were curtained off areas, presumably where attendees were getting up to kinky activities. The crack of a paddle hitting flesh and the cry of a submissive broke the genial atmosphere. But nobody batted an eye or evinced the least bit of interest. If they were, in fact, intrigued, they would continue to make small talk, then excuse themselves and head over to the place from which the noise had come. The people in attendance at this event were invited guests, experienced with the concept and presentation of public kink.

Since we were already moving, I steered us in the direction of some beautiful sounds of supplication and distress coming from the nearest curtained area with several people gathered at the opening. They made space for us in a communal movement.

On his knees in the middle of the floor, with his wrists bound at his back with rope and a ball gag in his mouth, a young man gazed with rapt attention at the woman standing before him. His cock was confined in a clear polycarbonate cock cage.

"Everyone, this is Jamie. Jamie, say hello to everyone." The woman with whom Jamie was so entranced waved her hand in a gentle arc over the crowd of onlookers.

Jamie did as she'd asked, his words distorted by the gag.

The Domme was of average height, but her sense of bearing and her avant-garde appearance gave her the presence of someone taller. She was beautiful, with deep brown eyes and skin a shade or two lighter. Her close-cropped hair hugged her head in tight curls. She wore snug black jeans, black suede ankle boots with a sharp heel and a tunic top of some glittering metallic fabric with the sleeves rolled up. On her hands were delicate black leather gloves that stopped just at the edge of her narrow wrists.

"Get up."

Jamie struggled to his feet, almost falling but recovering himself.

"Good boy," the Domme said. "Now, bend yourself over this table, so that we can all see your gorgeous backside."

Jamie mumbled something behind the gag that sounded like, "Yes, Mistress," and proceeded to curl his lithe body over the nearby metal folding table, spreading his legs as quite a few people gasped, now that they could see the base of a tempered glass anal plug.

"Nice," I said to Vincent, and glanced at Matteo, who seemed transfixed by the sight. "What do you think, boys? Maybe I should have caged and plugged you."

Vincent and Matteo exchanged a look.

"I'm going to remove your gag now, Jamie," the Domme said to her captive submissive.

I glanced at the name plate affixed to the curtain.

Mistress Slade.

Whether Slade was her first or last name, I had no clue. But I appreciated her showmanship.

Once the gag had been removed and her slave had thanked her for the honor of being free of it, Mistress Slade gave his ass a sharp spank, the noise echoing through the space.

"Are you having fun, Jamie?"

"Yes, Mistress."

"Do you like to show off, my little cabbage?"

"Yes, Mistress."

"Do you have a" — she ran her gloved hands over the globes of Jamie's behind — "a spectacular ass?"

"Yes, Mistress."

Laughter filled the space. I could attest that Jamie did indeed have a spectacular ass.

"Let's show everyone how that spectacular ass performs, shall we?"

Jamie groaned and shuddered. "Yes, Mistress."

"Be still. You shall remain motionless, while I withdraw this plug and insert it again. Every time it goes inside you, I want you to count."

"Yes, Mistress."

"*Bon.* On commence."

"*Oui, Maitresse.*"

Why does a soupçon of French words and phrases give a kink event that little bit of je ne sais quois?

I found Vincent's hand and threaded my fingers with his as Mistress Slade took hold of the base of the plug and pulled. As the glass device emerged from his slicked hole, Jamie made pitiful, vulnerable noises. The thing was wide — wider than I'd supposed — and long enough to fill him most thoroughly. People in the crowd gasped again as it popped out, and Jamie's shiny ring retracted.

I felt a shudder go through Vincent as we watched Mistress Slade poke the toy at Jamie's entrance then push it carefully in again, to the delight of the captive audience. Jamie groaned as the object spread him and lodged inside once more. "One. *Un,*" he said in a subdued voice.

Mistress Slade commended her obedient slave. "Excellent." She wiggled the plug to draw forth more sounds of delight from her charge, before tugging it out again, to the obvious pleasure of the breathless audience. This time, when the plug came out, Jamie whined with apparent agony. Either he was overacting or he genuinely despised feeling empty.

"Shhh. *Ca suffit*. That's enough. It's going back in, but you'll need to use your manners."

"*Oui, Maitresse. Puis j'avoir le jouet de neuveau?*"

"And in English?"

"Yes, Mistress. May I have the toy again?"

"If you say the magic word."

"Please, Mistress. *S'y vous plait, Maitresse.*"

"*Oui, vous pouvez.*" Mistress Slade winked at us, then took her attention back to Jamie. "Yes, you may."

The procedure was repeated many times to the delight of the group and to the enjoyment of Jamie, who seemed to love being humiliated in public and became more and more agitated and aroused as the event progressed. Finally, Mistress Slade settled the toy inside her boy and had him turn around to face us. His hair was disheveled and his cheeks were flushed bright red — with embarrassment or desire, I wasn't sure. Probably plenty of both.

"*Bon. Ouvre tes yeux*. Open your eyes. If you can keep them open, Jamie, I will set you free and allow you to orgasm."

Immediately, Jamie's eyes flashed wide. They rested on an object in the distance as Mistress Slade produced a key and removed the cage from the young man's genitals.

"Oh, hello," I said, licking my lips. Vincent was hypnotized by what was happening and I had to release his hand because it had become so sweaty and hot. Mistress Slade removed her kid gloves and took her slave's penis in her bare hand, teasing him with ease to a full erection and crooning indignities in a soft, smoky voice.

"I like to fuck you with the toy in front of so many people. You are such a lovely object to play with. Your little cock is such a delight to tease."

By now, Jamie was struggling. I didn't know how long he'd been caged, but by the looks of him, it must have been a good while. He appeared ready to burst out of his skin as his mistress fondled his cock and balls.

"Do you want to have an orgasm? Hmm? Do you want Mistress Slade to make you come in front of all these people?"

"Yes, Mistress. Please, *Maitresse! S'y vous plait! Je besoin de venir…*"

"Very well. Come when you like. But if it's not in the next couple of seconds I will need to move along. There are other boys waiting their turn."

"Yes, Mistress!" Jamie panted, as she began a focused jerking of his cock that caused him to emit the most delicious sounds of pleasure. Every time his eyes fell closed, Mistress Slade said *"Ouvert!"* in a forceful tone, and Jamie obeyed — until with a loud cry, he shuddered and spurted streams of jizz over the floor while the audience watched with avid fascination.

I brought my hands together in one loud clap. Mistress Slade gave me a small bow as the crowd took up the applause, and Jamie suffered the aftershocks of an intense orgasm.

"Well, that was…" Vincent murmured.

"Exceptional," I finished.

"Delicious," Matteo agreed.

I grinned at him. "Ready to be put on display?"

Matteo cleared his throat. "Now?"

"Yes, now. What's the problem?"

"I'm…hard."

"All the better."

I grinned at him as Mistress Slade had Jamie tidy up the mess he'd made and the observers exited the curtained space to move onto the next spectacle. "Why don't you take off your clothes here while I introduce myself to the Mistress. Vincent, gather Matteo's things and we'll have them checked with our coats."

"Of course, Sir," Vincent said, his voice catching. He'd been affected by Jamie and Mistress Slade, I could tell.

I walked over to the intimidating Domme. Her delicate fingers cupped Jamie's clean-shaven jaw as she whispered to him and held his gaze. He nodded and smiled. Then she smiled and kissed him with astonishing gentleness.

"I'm sorry to interrupt," I said, "but I wanted to tell you how much I enjoyed the performance."

Mistress Slade slid her dark gaze to me while Jamie fluttered his eyelashes, not daring to look at me directly.

"Thank you so much. You are?"

"Nic Walker," I said, holding out my hand. "I'm a friend of Daphne's."

"*Oui, je sais.* I know. I've heard so much about you. It's wonderful to finally meet you."

I smiled and put my hands in my pockets, nodding at Jamie. "He's lovely."

She regarded her sweet slave with indulgence. "Such a good boy. He does so love a public performance."

"I can see that. May I address him?"

"Of course." Mistress Slade touched Jamie under the chin to get him to look up. "Jamie, this is Nic." She turned to me. "You may touch him if you like."

"Thank you." I walked closer and stood in front of Jamie, who watched me with care, caution, and appropriate deference. "Hi, Jamie."

His eyes met mine. "Hi."

"You are very beautiful and docile."

"Thank you, Sir."

"Do you enjoy pleasing your *maitresse*?" I knew the answer, but I wanted to hear him say it.

"*Oui, monsieur. Plus que tout.* More than anything."

I smiled and put a finger under his chin, as his mistress had done, tilting his face so I could see it from all angles. He could have been a cover model. I didn't think he knew how pretty he was.

"Hmm," I said. "Make sure you get a rest between performances."

He nodded. "My mistress takes very good care of me." He glanced at Mistress Slade without moving his head.

"If you like, while we are taking a break, you may use this space," Mistress Slade said, eyeing Vincent and Matteo. "You have two lovely boys with you, although one may be a girl, *non*? He is, how does one say it, very androgynous. *Je pense qu'il est magnifique.*"

I smiled, proud of both my subs this evening. "Thank you. Vincent is very fluid when it comes to his gender. But he prefers he/him pronouns, nonetheless."

"Noted."

"I think we will take over this space while you and Jamie have a rest. I'm sure I can come up with something for them to do."

By this time, Matteo had finished removing his clothes, and stood beside Vincent with his head bowed and his hands behind his back, like Jamie.

Jamie seemed mesmerized by Matteo and couldn't tear his eyes away from our dark, brooding 'boy' with his swarthy build and solid erection.

"*Maitresse, puis je le servir?*" Jamie asked.

Mistress Slade cocked her head. "But you need to rest, *mon petit*."

"*Je vais bien. Je me peux reposer apres.*"

"*Une moment.*" Mistress Slade looked my way and rested her hip on the edge of the table. "Jamie would like to suck off the naked one, if you don't mind."

Matteo's head shot up. His lips parted and a puff of air came out. Then he remembered himself and bowed his head, shifting on his feet as a shudder went through him.

"Hmm-m. That depends on Matteo. Let me ask him, since this wasn't a part of our preparation."

I moved close and put my mouth to Matteo's ear. "Please don't feel obligated, Matteo. But if you'd like Jamie to give you a blow job, I don't have a problem with it."

Matteo nodded, his gaze on his own feet.

"Yes, please," Matteo said, choking on his words.

Vincent had gathered up Matteo's clothes but hesitated, his gaze moving between Jamie and Matteo.

"Go on, Vincent. We'll wait until you get back," I assured him. I turned to Jamie and Mistress Slade. "In the meantime, I'll ensure he remains interested."

I didn't think that would be a problem, but I wrapped my fingers around Matteo's erection anyway as I exchanged small talk with Mistress Slade. Matteo's gaze remained fixed on Jamie as I worked him like it was an afterthought. His muscles bunched and his lips parted in the anticipation of what was to come.

When Vincent returned, instead of instructing Jamie to begin, Mistress Slade cleared her throat and held up her finger.

"*Attend.*" She glanced at Vincent. "If it is all right with you, I would like to kiss your gender fluid boy, as he is very beautiful."

The question caught me off guard. But it was only a kiss.

I smiled at Vincent. "Do you consent? If you're not comfortable, I won't be upset."

Vincent blushed and nodded. "I'm okay with it," he said, glancing at Mistress Slade.

It was turning me on. This whole scenario and chance encounter was making me crazy. It had been so long since I'd attended a fetish event, and I was out of practice.

Mistress Slade laughed, a sound like bells. "He's okay with it? *Mon dieu.*"

"Would you like Mistress Slade to kiss you, Vincent?"

"Very much, Sir. If she pleases."

"*Merveilleuse!*" Mistress Slade said, approaching Vincent as if he were an exotic wild animal.

She stepped close to him and took his chin in her gloved hand. He echoed her slow smile as they leaned close and touched lips in a tentative kiss. Mistress Slade closed her eyes and leaned into it. She was gentle and cautious, giving Vincent a taste and taking one herself. When she pulled away, they held each other's gazes for a few seconds, then Mistress Slade sighed.

"*Bon. Ca suffit.*" She turned to me. "Thank you so much."

"You're very welcome."

"Now, Jamie, if you'd like to come forward and use your well-developed skills on this gorgeous submissive, I have no objection."

"Yes, Mistress. Thank you, Mistress."

Jamie moved forward and dropped to his knees before Matteo as I aimed Matteo's cock at the smaller man's lips.

"There you are. Get him off, if you can."

"Yes, Sir," Jamie said, licking his lips. He leaned forward, glancing upward at Matteo's soft green eyes before swallowing the poor man to the hilt.

Matteo choked on a groan and gazed at the ceiling as Jamie went wild on his dick. Mistress Slade watched her young slave take Matteo apart in a matter of moments.

When Matteo was close, he turned to tell me. Jamie pulled off and closed his eyes, pressing his lips together as he used his hand to finish Matteo off, aiming his cock so Matteo's hot bursts of spunk landed on Jamie's face. When Matteo was finished, Jamie grinned.

"*Merci,*" he said, wiping at his defiled complexion with the back of a trembling hand.

Chapter Eight

Mistress Slade swiped Jamie's face with a cloth, then approached Vincent and me.

"*Mon dieu*," she said to Vincent. "Your tongue is the answer to my every desire. It's a shame I just get to have it in my mouth."

Vincent smiled. "You are very tasty, Mistress. I couldn't help myself."

We exchanged a glance.

"By the way, these pants." She clicked her tongue, her gaze stroking over the snug, metallic material. "They are almost indecent."

"Perfect for a play party," I stated.

Mistress Slade smiled. "Indeed. The boots, too. *Parfait*."

Mistress Slade's gaze landed on the plum-colored Docs.

"Yes." She sighed and stepped back from my beautiful boy. "*Alors*. I must let you go. Thank you for allowing me the merest taste of your beauty."

I placed a hand on Mistress Slade's shoulder.

"If you would permit me?" I said, leaning in and waiting for a smile before I brought my lips to hers. We kissed for a long moment, my nose picking up hints of pachouli and incense.

When we parted, I glanced at Vincent, who seemed entranced to see me kissing a woman. Before *him*, it had been only women, and now I was partnered with *two* men. Body parts made no difference to me, in the end.

I kissed Mistress Slade's cheek and squeezed her hand. "We should move on. Bye, Jamie," I said, giving the young man a wave. He was tidying himself up and peeking at Matteo, who stood watching.

I snapped my fingers. "Matteo. Come."

He immediately obeyed.

"Sir, I—" Matteo began.

"Yes? Are you all right?"

"Yes, Sir. But am I to be led around naked all evening?"

"If it suits me."

His body vibrated as he chuckled, and I glanced behind me to see him smile.

"Yes, Sir."

I raised his hand to my lips and kissed the back of it. "Do you know how proud you make me?"

"I like to please you."

"You do please me. Normally it's by making delicious meals for us. At the moment it's by allowing me to show you off." I glanced down his naked body. "All of you."

"Yes, Sir."

Vincent took Matteo's other hand and whispered, "Me, too."

Matteo blushed and looked infinitely pleased. "Well, then," he said.

Matteo was a seasoned submissive and comfortable with public nudity. It didn't take long for the goings-on around us to cause a renewal of lust and the return of a sizeable erection. We were the subject of much interest, with Matteo unclothed, Vincent in his metallic jeans and purple boots and me in my velvet jacket and leather pants.

We watched a young woman bent over a table and soundly paddled by her male Dom. And two young men in intricate shibari harnesses, suspended from a frame in a sixty-nine position give each other pleasure to the point of completion.

That one earned much applause from the crowd of watchers.

Next, mummification and forced orgasms, flogging and finally, a delicious red-headed boy in the stocks who was the subject of much admiration as he was teased and caned by his equally attractive, blond Dom.

The Dom wielded the tool with care, because such a powerful implement could overwhelm a submissive if wielded without a certain level of skill. I didn't use them myself, but they had their place. The cane, in this instance, was a slim rattan object with a black handle — springy and would deal quite the sting, but not the harsh thump intrinsic to a heavier material.

The Dom looked to be about my age, with as slim a build as his boy in the stocks. I say 'boy' but, of course, the red-headed darling looked to be in his early twenties. He squealed each time a strike of the cane landed on his pert buttocks, and it left a bright red mark for several moments. The boy's Dom would give him three spaced strikes, then massage and soothe him, then slip a finger or two up his ass, to a lovely auditory soundtrack from his submissive, then deal three more strikes — and so on.

Vincent shuddered as he watched. His gaze met mine and his lips parted.

"You can speak if you want. Both of you. No need to stay silent as long as you are respectful."

"That's so damn hot," Vincent murmured, his gaze on the redheaded submissive.

"Yes," I agreed. I cocked my head. "Would you be interested in trying something like that sometime?" I was curious.

Vincent blanched. "I don't think so, Sir. But I like to watch. He seems to get off on it."

Indeed. The redhead had an impressive, leaking boner that didn't seem to flag, no matter how much he protested the pain.

When the Dom was done, he released his boy from the wooden contraption. The red-headed submissive fell to his knees at the Dom's feet and proceeded to kiss and lick his boots in an excess of thanks for the abuse.

"Enough. Stand." The Dom's voice held strength and confidence.

The boy got up, trembling and covered with a sheen of sweat, before his Dom, who gazed at the crowd.

"Would anyone like to reward my boy? He deserves something special after that performance."

I glanced at Matteo, who licked his lips and inclined his head. I raised my hand.

"May I offer Matteo, Sir? I'd like to put him to work, and your boy would benefit from his skills."

The blond Dom assessed both of us, then nodded. "Bring him forward."

I stepped forward and guided Matteo to stand before the Dom. It was a relief, after all the heavy shit we'd dealt with recently, to be in a situation where we were simply Dom and sub.

The Dom introduced himself. "My name is Master Cameron. My boy's name is Arthur." He looked Matteo over with undisguised lust. "You can give him a reward for good behavior, if I may call upon you after."

Matteo glanced my way. I nodded. He bowed his head before Master Cameron. "I am at your service, Master Cameron."

As a condition of entry into this exclusive event, participants had been required to send in recent results of STD testing, to keep intimate interactions as safe as possible. Still, like Mistress Slade had probably instructed Jamie, I'd told Matteo and Vincent to avoid swallowing semen, if it became relevant. The risks of contracting HIV from oral sex were low, but I didn't want to risk more than we had to. And also, sex was more fun when it was messy.

"Excellent. Make Arthur come while I watch. Then you can service me."

Matteo cleared his throat. "Yes, Sir."

It was thrilling to watch Matteo drop to his knees and proceed to use his extensive skills on the red-headed boy, who kept his hands clasped behind his neck and made the most scrumptious noises.

It didn't take long for the red-headed submissive to utter a long groan and finish. Matteo didn't swallow, but let Arthur's spunk dribble down his chin, spitting the rest onto the floor.

"Here, Arthur. Clean that up," Master Cameron said, passing a cloth to the dazed redhead. He turned to me.

"Are you enjoying the party?"

"Yes. We haven't been to one in a long time."

"Do you live locally?"

"Yes. You?"

"Montreal. We're down here for the week."

My eyes widened with surprise. "You live in Montreal, but you came to Ottawa for a play party?"

He laughed. "Yeah, that does sound strange. My friend is one of the organizers. And we have other friends in town. You are?"

"Oh, sorry. I'm Nic. And this is Matteo and" — I gestured to Vincent, who stood quietly, watching Arthur recover from his encounter with Matteo — "Vincent."

Master Cameron took my hand in a firm grip. "I'm very pleased to meet you and your beautiful subs." His eyes gobbled up Vincent. "This one's very pretty, like Arthur."

"Thank you. Arthur is adorable."

"Now, I would like to take advantage of the table just here, so I can rest and watch your boy, Matteo, swallow my cock before all of these people."

I hadn't realized how large of a crowd had gathered until Master Cameron referenced it. But there were a lot of people observing as he perched himself on the table, then lay down on his back, with his legs hanging off the platform, and undid his pants, pulling out a substantial and erect, circumcised cock.

He stroked himself as he beckoned to Matteo, who moved forward and stood between Master Cameron's knees, his chest rising and falling as he gazed on his target.

"What are you waiting for, boy?" Master Cameron said with a smirk, tracking Matteo with eager eyes.

Matteo tossed his head to move the fall of hair off his forehead, then leaned, braced his hands on either side of Master Cameron and bent to the Dom's thick cock.

"Oh, yes. That's very good," Master Cameron said after a few moments of Matteo's attention. He threaded his fingers in Matteo's thick hair, then sighed, gazing down to where my partner was giving him some very good head.

Matteo made a whimper of pleasure as he went after Master Cameron's orgasm with the eagerness of a pro. Matteo wasn't often playful and impulsive like Vincent, but he was persistent and thorough. He knew what to do to get other men off, and he went at it like it was his sole duty—which it did seem to be, at the moment.

Vincent, Arthur and I watched avidly, along with a host of others, as Master Cameron became undone before our very eyes.

This was more enjoyable than I'd expected. As Matteo deep-throated him, he closed his eyes and whimpered. When his eyes opened, his gaze landed on mine. "Nic Walker, you are a lucky man."

I inclined my head in acknowledgment. "I know I am, Master Cameron."

Master Cameron crooked his finger at Vincent. "I'd like to kiss your other boy before I come," he said.

I looked at Vincent with my eyes raised. He nodded, his face flushed and his breaths coming quick.

"Off you go," I said, and Vincent approached Master Cameron and bent over the table to touch his lips to the older man's.

Master Cameron brought his hand up behind Vincent's neck to keep him still as they deepened their kiss. Then he pulled away to warn Matteo of his impending orgasm.

Matteo pulled off and stood still as Master Cameron jerked off, globs of spunk raining above the table and landing on the Dom's belly and chest.

When the aftershocks had finished, Master Cameron tidied up with a cloth, and thanked Matteo for a job well done.

"Ooooh, fuck," he said. "That was just what I needed."

I stepped forward to let Matteo know how pleased I was. Before I could step away, Master Cameron took my arm.

"One moment, if you don't mind, Nic Walker."

We gazed at one another. Part of me was annoyed at being detained, but another part of me was intrigued by Master Cameron. He was only a bit taller than me. "Yes?"

Master Cameron gave me a broad smile. The skin beside his eyes crinkled with pleasure. "Thanks for allowing me to use Matteo. I wonder if you and Vincent would like use mine."

"Oh," I said, not expecting that. I glanced at Arthur, who stood beside a short-haired woman who had placed a blanket over his shoulders and was speaking to him in a barely audible tone.

"No, not Arthur," Master Cameron explained. "I have another boy with me, and he has been waiting very patiently for his turn."

Master Cameron slid off the table and gestured to my right, where a young man in nothing but a leather collar and a cock cage was being led over by a different woman, who bowed and gave Master Cameron the boy's lead.

"This beautiful young thing is Finn." Master Cameron shrugged as I stared at the man's shoulder-length hair, that was an even darker shade of red than Arthur's. Finn's elfin features were spattered with dark freckles. "I have a thing for redheads. What I can I say?"

I smiled. "You don't need to explain. I admire the aesthetic myself."

"Finn," Master Cameron ejected, causing the boy's head to jerk up. "Show Mr. Walker your teeth and tongue."

Finn's blue eyes flashed irritation for a moment, then he obediently opened his mouth and stuck out his tongue. His white teeth were clean and straight, his gums and tongue pink and appealing.

"That's not necessary," I said with a wave of my hand. "I know you wouldn't offer me a boy with substandard…orifices."

Master Cameron laughed. "No. I certainly wouldn't."

I glanced at Vincent. "Well? What do you think? Want to take Finn for a spin?"

Vincent did a double take at the young man, then gazed questions at me. "I—beg your pardon? Sir?"

I took his elbow and pulled him aside. "I don't mean to blindside you, but remember we were going to try to explore different roles and dynamics? If you want, you can have a turn being the one in control. Master Cameron will let you play with Finn if you want to. If you don't, I'll put him through his paces. And I can Dom him alongside you, if you're nervous."

Vincent took a shuddering breath. "Do you think it's all right with Finn?"

I smiled. I could tell Vincent was on board. How could he not be, looking at the stunning redhead with the captivating complexion. "I'll check with Master Cameron."

Master Cameron chortled at my question. "Finn lives for this sort of thing. But I'll ask him if you want." He turned to the freckled young man. "Finn, do you want to be Vincent's blue-eyed slut? Nic's, too?" he said, pointing at me.

Finn's blue eyes drifted from me to Vincent and back again. I noticed them fix on the hem of Vincent's black shirt where a bit of his treasure-trail could be seen.

"Sure," Finn said, with a casualness that took me by surprise, but Master Cameron didn't react as if this informal address were unexpected.

"Good boy," Master Cameron said.

Finn had a deeper voice than I'd expected. It gave him the stature of someone older and contrasted with his youthful, almost fey, appearance. I did love a paradox, especially one wrapped in such an alluring package.

I had to think fast. I wanted to do so much, but we only had a short period of time to enjoy him."

"What does Finn like?" I asked, circling the boy and examining him from every angle.

"Oh, a little pain goes a long way—spanking, nipple torture, pinching, slapping. He likes to be controlled. And humiliated, as long as it doesn't go too far."

"That's perfect." I exchanged a glance with Vincent, who looked as if he were about to unwrap a surprise gift on Christmas morning. "Let's put him up on the table for now."

"Front or back?" Master Cameron asked.

"Vincent?"

"Back. May we take off the cage, Master Cameron?"

Master Cameron produced a small key from his pocket and handed it to Vincent. "Be my guest. Boy hasn't come in three weeks, though, just so you know. You'll be playing with fire. I apologize if he's unable to last long."

"That's not a problem, Master Cameron," I assured him. "I'm used to boys who struggle with control." I glanced at Vincent.

It was a bit of a dig, and he stuck out his tongue at me.

"Don't think I won't put that tongue to good use." I grinned.

"With all due respect, Sir, in the capacity of a fellow-Dom, I can do whatever I like with my tongue," Vincent replied.

I raised my brows, pleased to see him so cocky. *Challenge accepted.*

"All right, then. What do you want to do with him, Vincent?"

Vincent gazed down at Finn, who lay spread out on the table with his legs dangling, equally focused on Vincent. Finn's cock fought the bars of the cage as his chest rose and fell with anticipation, and Finn's blue eyes—almost the same shade as Vincent's—regarded him with expectation.

Vincent moved close to the table and feasted his eyes on the young man's lithe body. "Hello, Finn."

Finn blinked slowly. "Hello, Vincent."

Vincent gave Finn a soft smile and picked up the boy's hand where it rested motionless on the table. He examined Finn's smooth palm, turning it over in his grasp and placing a delicate kiss in the middle.

Finn gasped. "Yeah, you're hot. You gonna hurt me?"

The way he said it made it more of a request than an honest question. I had to put my hand in front of my mouth so as not to betray my amusement. But I caught Master Cameron's eyes just after he'd rolled them.

Vincent glanced my way for reassurance. I motioned him to continue, since he was doing just fine. I was more than willing to step back and watch him take over, intrigued by his confidence, hoping he'd still be willing to be my devoted servant most of the time, but not opposed to the idea of his occasional foray into dominance at a rare public event, especially when it involved such a willing, beautiful subject as Finn.

Vincent released Finn's hand and used the tiny key Master Cameron had given him to unlock the device on the boy's genitals. As he removed it, Finn's cock filled without any touch until it reared against the young man's belly. It was smaller than average, but I didn't think Vincent cared about that, especially since it seemed to work with Finn's overall aesthetic. Besides, this fairy creature made up for his diminutive size with the enthusiasm of his gaze. He stared flames at Vincent, clearly hoping that my alluring partner in the metallic jeans and tight top might give him what he wanted.

But Vincent handed the cage to Master Cameron and proceeded to ignore Finn's raging erection as he spent a good amount of time touching the beautiful boy everywhere else with an almost reverent attention. Finn's gaze followed Vincent's as Vincent examined every inch of him.

The people who had gathered watched with undisguised interest.

A young woman in a snug, flowered red dress moved up beside me.

"He's so beautiful," she said, with an amiable smile, then held out her hand. "I'm Leslie."

I glanced beside me, irritated to be disturbed. But when I took in Leslie's convivial, unguarded expression, I relaxed. "Yes. He looks like a pretty fairy about to be debauched."

"Oh, no. I meant the one in the purple boots. Is he with you?"

I assessed her, but she didn't seem to be asking out of anything above curiosity.

"Yes, he is. Vincent and I and Matteo are together." I gestured to where Matteo stood behind me on the other side. "Vincent generally takes a submissive role, but I thought he'd like to play with Finn in a more dominant way. I'm interested to see what he'll do."

"Oooh, so am I," Leslie said, turning to watch the tableau before us.

Vincent was now playing with Finn's nipples, as Finn squirmed and gasped and Master Cameron chuckled.

"You've found his Achilles' heel, Vincent. That boy's nipples are so sensitive he may just explode from that alone."

Vincent regarded Master Cameron with curiosity. "You think he could orgasm from this?"

As if providing his answer, Finn groaned and shuddered, one hand moving to his arching cock.

"Finn!" Master Cameron said, in such a stern and loud tone that Finn immediately moved his hand to above his head.

"I'm sorry, Master Cameron."

"Hands off the goods. Just because Vincent removed the cage doesn't mean you can touch yourself. You know the rules."

"Yes, Master Cameron."

Master Cameron exchanged a glance with Vincent and ambled over to Finn. "Would you like some help keeping your hands off the goods, little fairy boy?"

Finn frowned, as if the reference to fairies offended him. Then he seemed to think better of it and sighed, "Yes, Master Cameron."

Master Cameron moved to stand at the head of the table, clasping Finn's hands in his, keeping Finn's arms stretched over his head. He held him there and nodded to Vincent. "Continue…and let's see."

Vincent smiled, knowing full well what if felt like to be so sensitive. He went back and forth between Finn's nipples, tickling and teasing, pinching and scratching, until the boy was a squirming, panting mess of desire.

The redhead fought against Master Cameron's hold. "Oh fuck. Fuck. Stop. I mean, no. Don't stop. Oooooh."

"Do you have a safeword, Finn?" Vincent said.

Finn gazed at him with desperation and groaned, twitching on the table.

"It's 'freckles'," Master Cameron said.

Vincent grinned. "Uh-huh. Say it if you need to, Finn. Otherwise I'm going to keep doing what I'm doing."

Finn groaned again in seeming agony but didn't say anything more. He gazed at Master Cameron and struggled in his grasp, his body moving on the table as if caught in an irresistible current. His dangling legs jerked and swayed as Vincent kept up his relentless torment. He seemed to have resigned himself to his submission now.

I met Vincent's heated gaze over the table. He licked his lips, and it was easy to see how aroused he was. He swallowed and twisted Finn's nipple in a cruel way.

"That's such a desperate cock. It wants to let go, but it's not getting what it needs," Vincent crooned, in tones that almost sounded bored.

Finn moaned again, his cock jerking and clear fluid surging from the glans.

Vincent pinched the other nipple just as hard then leaned down to blow on the wetness there.

"Ahhh! Fuck!" Finn sputtered.

When Vincent bent to take Finn's other nipple into his mouth, the boy arched up, screaming as his penis ululated and thick white streams of semen spurted over his pale, freckled belly.

A communal gasp went through the crowd. Vincent didn't seem aware. He continued to suck one nipple and pinch the other. He relinquished the boy when Finn's spasms quieted down. He gazed upon the results of his work and slid his right hand down to glide his fingers through the hot spunk on the boy's stomach.

The audience fell into a round of applause, and Master Cameron laughed.

"Nicely done, Vincent. Have you ever played such a fine instrument?"

Vincent inclined his head, reaching out to smooth a finger over Finn's wet nipple, as if he could hardly keep from touching it. Finn moaned and regarded Vincent with trepidation and excitement.

"Nic taught me to play the piano. But this is much more fun."

The audience laughed.

Vincent shot a gleeful gaze my way, and I made a small bow.

"You are excellent at both. Well done, my darling."

Poor Matteo stood, ignored and hard as a rock beside me, gazing at Vincent like he was a gorgeous revelation.

Chapter Nine

Attending the kink party had been a wise decision. For days afterward, we couldn't stop thinking about it, talking about it. It rejuvenated our interest in doing scenes together, and now I alternated with Vincent and Matteo in terms of running things. They both preferred to sub, but the occasional foray into dominance wasn't a problem.

I praised Vincent for his ability to take on the dominant role in public. I'd worried he'd be shy at the play party, but he'd exceeded all of my expectations.

I had resolved to make a continuous effort to include Juno and Charles in our lives, as well as Daphne, although she was busy with Alexander and didn't have much free time.

Matteo kept close tabs on Zarah, making sure she was all right. It looked as though he had frightened her ex, Dennis, enough that he stayed out of Zarah's way. According to Matteo, she'd enlisted a male friend to go pick up the things she wanted from the house. It wasn't much. She intended to make a fresh start. It was a relief in the sense that she'd gotten away, her ex didn't know she was pregnant, none of his loser friends knew and she had us and a circle of other people who could help with whatever she needed.

Matteo was still reeling from the discovery that Zarah did indeed want him in her life again, that she'd been gaslighted into excluding him in the first place and that he had a grandchild on the way.

"Life is crazy, huh?" I said to him.

"It can be. I can't regret what happened, because I may never have ended up making my way to you and Vincent if I'd had more demands on my time. So, yes, I'm thrilled I have you both, and now I get Zarah and her baby, too."

I circled his neck with my arm and bent him to my level, kissing his head. "And we get all that, too."

He eyed me curiously. "Are you going to be okay with a baby around?"

I blinked. "Well, I mean, it's not going to live here, right?" I started to feel a bit queasy.

He laughed. "No. But I may want to look after my grandchild for an occasional weekend, so I can give Zarah a break."

I thought about what it would mean to have an infant around on an occasional basis. It wasn't something I was all that excited about. But if it meant making Matteo happy and helping Zarah out, I could put up with it.

"Hell, Matteo, if you'd told me three years ago I'd be living with two men and parenting a teenager, I would have laughed in your face and told you that was impossible. But I've learned to take what life throws at me and be grateful."

The door pushed open as Taylor came in from outside and clapped his gloved hands together. "Fuck, it's cold out there." He dropped his bag and toed off his boots. "What's for supper, Matteo?"

"Your favorite."

"Oh, fuck yes." Taylor fist-pumped the air and took off his jacket.

To my surprise he came over and kissed me on the cheek.

I gave him a look. "What was that for?"

He shrugged. "For housing and feeding me...and being an awesome Dad."

"O-kay. What's brought this on?"

"Don't know. Just, things are going great, y'know."

I grinned, pleased to see Taylor so content. "How's Riley?"

Taylor blushed, a rare enough occurrence. "Riley is delicious."

"Oh my," I said, clearing my throat.

"Well, you did ask." Taylor could hardly contain his glee.

"Perhaps you don't need any supper," Matteo said.

"Man cannot live on...man...alone. Besides, I've, uh" — Taylor tried not to smile — "worked up an appetite."

I couldn't help laughing at Taylor's cheek, but I shook my head to show I didn't necessarily approve of a young man spending the entire afternoon in flagrante delecto with his lover.

Oh, who am I kidding? Of course I did. I made my hand into a fist and held it out.

Taylor stared at my hand. "Oh my God."

Matteo stopped walking toward the kitchen and glanced behind him.

"Shhh. No sudden movements. Nic wants me to fist-bump him. What the fuck is happening?"

The hand that had been a fist shot out and clamped down on Taylor's earlobe.

"Ow! Fuck!"

I twisted it so that he had to bend in a strange way and smiled down at him.

"Don't make fun of your elders. It's not attractive."

"I'm not trying to be attractive to y— Ow! Help, I need a safeword!"

I let him go. He took a step back and rubbed at his ear.

"Jesus. Old people sure have tempers."

I surged to my feet, but Taylor held up a hand and immediately backtracked.

"I'm sorry. I'm sorry."

"Behave yourself or you'll be sent to bed with no supper."

"That *would* be tragic. Consider me behaved." Taylor went and cozied up to Matteo. "You still love me, don't you, Daddy?"

Matteo simply turned his head and planted a soft kiss on Taylor's scalp, while Taylor flashed me a narrow-eyed gaze.

"Don't forget I have a drawer full of wooden paddles in the basement," I said.

"Who could forget that? But you wouldn't waste your talents on little me. Plus, it would be mondo weird since you like to do it to Vincent."

I gave him an evil look. "That's true. I'll have to come up with another form of punishment."

Taylor gazed up at Matteo with pouting lips. "Matteo, Daddy Nic is being mean to me."

Matteo snorted. "Daddy Nic is being very patient with you. Stop being a brat. Go upstairs and get cleaned up for supper."

It was hilarious to hear mild-mannered Matteo reach the end of his patience. I tried to keep the smile off my face.

"Fine. I get nothing but grief in this place." Taylor shook his head exaggeratedly, walking backward to the stairs. "Why do I even put up with you all?"

"Matteo's cooking," I suggested.

He finger-gunned me before grinning and heading upstairs with the agility of the youth he was. "That must be it."

"Are you going to Riley's later?"

"Nah, I want to see Juno and Charles," he said, then scratched at his neck. "Also, Riley's mom's coming over to bring him some leftover Christmas cake or something. We...uh, don't get along."

This was the first I'd heard of that. "Oh?"

"Yeah." Taylor shrugged. "She brings back bad memories." I raised my eyebrows and he said, "Talks about God a lot."

Now it made sense. "Oh. I see. Does it bother Riley?"

"A bit, but he's been moved out for a couple of years, and she hardly comes around anymore."

"Does she know he's gay?"

"Yes."

"Does she know he's seeing you?"

"Yes."

"Well. That's good, I suppose."

At that moment, the doorbell rang. Vincent answered it, a dishcloth in his hand. Outside were Juno and Charles, carrying a substantial and elaborate gift basket.

I peered around Vincent. "Goodness. Who's that for?"

Juno arched their brow. "It's for Taylor."

And all of a sudden Taylor was back, as if someone had blown a dog whistle.

"What?" Taylor said. "For me? Fuck, yeah!"

I stepped back as they entered the house, and Charles passed the basket to Taylor, who could barely contain his excitement.

"Thanks! Wow, look at all the goodies!"

"Yes. It's…excessive," I said, peering at the collection of items.

Juno narrowed their eyes at me. "I owe Taylor. His GoFundMe campaign has been a brilliant success."

"Well, that's wonderful. I suppose he does deserve it, then."

"Don't worry, Nic, I'll share," Taylor said, placing the cellophane-wrapped basket on the counter. "You know, you didn't have to bring me anything, Juno. I'm happy to help."

"I wanted to see your excitement when I brought it. At my age, that depth of emotion is elusive."

I rolled my eyes. "Oh, Juno, don't be so dramatic."

"Oh, Nic, I shall be as dramatic as I please."

I laughed. "What was I thinking?"

"Juno. Charles," Matteo greeted them with a smile.

"Matteo! How is the fabulous cook? You know, I envy Nic so much, having you in the kitchen and the bedroom whenever he pleases. I know you're talented in the kitchen, so I can only imagine how wonderful you are upstairs."

Matteo inclined his head. "My talent lies purely in my cooking skills."

"Oh no. Nic would not stand for less than perfection in the bedroom. Don't be modest."

I steered Juno into the living room. "You have Charles, who is quite delightful. And I've no doubt that if he can keep up with you, he must be very skilled indeed…in all sorts of things." I winked at the sweet young man who followed us.

"Well, yes, he is. You're right. Charles looks after me very well."

They sat on the sofa and pulled Charles onto their lap. Charles immediately dipped his head into the crook of Juno's neck and wrapped his arms around them, whispering his thanks at the high praise.

"Of course, I have Vincent to thank for Charles' latest accomplishment," Juno murmured.

Vincent raised his eyebrows. "Oh? What have I done?"

Juno narrowed a devilish gaze toward my boy. "You, my dear, have shown Charles that a teeny tiny metal cage is nothing to be afraid of."

All four gazes drifted to Charles' crotch.

"Is he — right now?" Vincent asked.

"Why, yes, he is, Vincent," Juno said.

"I don't know that 'like' is the right word, exactly," Charles said, his voice muffled in Juno's neck.

"Hmm-m, let me rephrase. He seems to tolerate being caged for the sake of going into such a heightened state of arousal that he can barely think straight. I've had to end his sessions ahead of schedule every time because the poor boy becomes hopelessly agitated. But he's getting better. We've been able to go longer. How long has it been this time?"

"A week." Charles drew back with a frown. "Juno, it's been a week! I just realized. You said you would —"

Juno gazed at Charles, non-plussed. "Well, I can't exactly remove it right now. You'll have to wait until we get home."

Charles looked crestfallen at Juno's words. He glanced at me and Vincent and Matteo, obviously mulling something over. Then he leaned down and whispered into Juno's ear.

"But, Charles —" Juno muttered with some exasperation.

Charles kept whispering, his hand clutching Juno's shirt with an intensity that spoke to the urgency of his predicament.

Finally, Juno turned to me. "Nic. May I take Charles upstairs for a moment?"

I knew what would happen upstairs. But I couldn't think of a reason to deny them.

"Of course you can. Take all the time you need."

"Thank you," Juno said. They urged Charles up off their lap and whispered something to him. Charles walked over and sank to his knees in front of me.

"Thank you, Nic. I am forever grateful."

Oh, for Heaven's sake. Does Juno need to make a production out of everything?

I stroked Charles' silky-soft hair. "You are a very good boy, Charles. You deserve to be rewarded."

Charles squirmed and coughed as Vincent fought a smile. He knew how it felt to be in such a state of pent-up desire that mere words could cause waves of delight.

"Thank you, Sir," Charles said, breaths coming fast. He managed to stand and take Juno's hand before being led up the staircase.

Vincent and Matteo and I exchanged a glance.

I shrugged. "Well, that shouldn't take long, at least. The poor kid is ripe for it."

I turned to Taylor, who had observed everything without a remark. He knew about this stuff, of course. You couldn't live in this house without being exposed to all the trivialities of various BDSM practices. "So, the Go Fund Me campaign for Juno's project is going well?"

Taylor grinned. "Yeah. I knew it would. They have so much support within the community, and sharing it this way, it's very easy for people to donate."

"Hmm. I would never have thought of it."

"Okay, Boomer."

I narrowed my eyes. "I'm not a Boomer. You take that back."

"Not officially, no. But the term has come to represent anyone older than forty."

I narrowed my eyes even more. "Taylor, I'm not —"

He shook his head. "Age doesn't matter, in fact. It's more of an…attitude."

I glared at him, prepared to argue, when Matteo and Vincent closed in on each side of me and kissed me sweetly on the cheeks.

"Never mind," Matteo said.

"Taylor, why don't you go check on supper?" Vincent suggested.

"Whatever."

Taylor made a gesture of futility and headed for the kitchen.

* * * *

At supper, Taylor refrained from further references to my age and relevancy. Charles and Juno seemed to share a silent secret, except that we all knew what it was.

"Now," I said, when we'd mostly finished eating. "We have to finalize the plans for our *Electric Dreams* extravaganza. It's only two weeks away."

"Shouldn't Daphne be here?" Juno suggested. "She was going to handle some of it."

"The catering has been put in place, as well as a sushi bar ordered for our slaves to display on their naked bodies," I said, gesturing to Vincent and Charles with a smile. "Daphne arranged all that."

Juno clapped their hands. "Excellent."

"Have you delivered all the artwork to the venue?"

"Yes, except for a couple of pieces I'm working on. But they will be ready."

"How many do we have?"

"Fifty pieces, in a range of sizes and prices. Mostly paintings but a few sculptures as well."

"Great!" I'd seen a couple of Juno's sculptures. They were original, with subtle erotic overtones, and vibrant, like their paintings. I was absolutely certain our event would be a success.

My cell phone rang just then in Daphne's exclusive ring tone.

"Hey, we're just going over the final details for the—"

"The place we were going to have it has backed out," Daphne said breathlessly.

"What? Are you serious?" I glanced at Juno. "But Juno's dropped off their artwork and everything."

Daphne sighed. "I know, I know. They were very apologetic. They said they'd help us relocate Juno's work."

"Well, fuck," I said.

"What is it?" Vincent asked, as his gaze met mine.

"The venue backed out. I'm just going to find out why," I said, putting Daphne on speaker.

Her annoyed voice filled the room. "Because, and I quote, 'They didn't realize it was anything more than an art show. When they understood there was kink involved, they didn't want to risk holding the event there.'"

"Goddammit," I groaned, waving my phone in the air. "This fucking city! Sometimes I think we should live in Toronto."

Vincent put a hand on my shoulder. "We'll find somewhere else."

"But it's only two weeks away!" Juno moaned, while Charles had resumed looking stressed.

"What about the place near the airport? They have the Sexapalooza show there every year," Matteo suggested.

"The EY Centre?" Taylor said. "Too expensive, and too popular. It's probably all booked up. We need a less well-known location, but central enough to draw a crowd.

"Yes, but it has to be big enough," Daphne said.

"I know, I know. I'm racking my brain," I said, pacing the room while the others looked on.

"What about the church?" Vincent suggested. "Where the play party was."

"Play party?" Juno said. "*What* play party?"

I held up my hand to quiet them.

"Maybe… We could see if they've been reserved for that weekend."

Juno looked at Charles. "We weren't invited to a play party." Charles shook his head to corroborate.

I considered the space. "That might just work. Daphne, leave it in our hands. I'll let you know if we confirm anything. Meanwhile, maybe let the caterers know there's been a change of location and we'll give them the new address as soon as we can."

We finished our meal while I fielded questions about the fetish party from Juno, then returned to the living area.

Vincent looked St. Brigid's up online, and we discovered they had two other rooms available, besides the large one we'd been in the other day.

"I'll call and see if we can book it," he said, disappearing into the kitchen with his phone.

Meanwhile, I searched for other possibilities, in case we couldn't.

The trouble with hosting a sex-positive event in a city like Ottawa was that there weren't a sizeable number of places that considered kink and kink-expression to be an actual part of healthy sexuality, even though all the recent research demonstrated it to be so. Ottawa was barely big enough to be called a city, but in some ways seemed like a smaller, sedate township. Heavily populated by government workers and their families, it had earned a reputation as a boring and conservative spot.

I knew that wasn't true, and that there was a vibrant, hidden world of kink underneath Ottawa's staid reputation. However, when one was looking to go public in a way that pushed boundaries, it presented some challenges. I should have anticipated there would be issues.

Juno had already finished two glasses of wine and was pouring another while Charles looked on with rising anxiety. They put the empty wine bottle on the coffee table.

"I hope you have more of this."

I sighed and picked it up.

"I'll check," I said, taking it into the kitchen where Vincent was involved in a phone conversation. I put the empty bottle on the counter and took a small bottle of San Pellegrino from the fridge, returning to the others.

"All I could find was this," I said pleasantly, putting it before them.

"You are a fucking bastard," Juno declared, eyeing the San Pel with distaste. "But Charles might want that."

"Yes, please," Charles said.

I passed the drink to him. "Vincent was negotiating with whomever was on the phone. So maybe they can fit us in."

"That's what he said," Taylor joked.

"Funny," Matteo commented, without laughing.

Taylor rolled his eyes. "You guys are no fun."

"Not when we need a venue for a show that is all but happening at this moment. No, we aren't," I commented, sinking into a chair with my second glass of wine.

"I'm sure you'll find something," Taylor remarked.

"Ah, the optimism of youth," I said.

"Well, usually you call me cynical, so I guess that's an improvement."

"Touché," I said. "Maybe it won't hurt to hope for the best."

"Why bother? Everything I've touched has gone to shit. Why should this be any different?" Juno lamented.

"Oh, give me a break. Your GoFundMe is already at twenty thousand," Taylor muttered.

Five heads swiveled toward Taylor.

"What?" Juno said.

"Say that again," I chirped.

"Whoa," Vincent exclaimed.

Matteo just chuckled.

"Here. See?" Taylor said, turning his laptop to show us. "You're going to have some commissions to do, but that shouldn't be difficult. They're small pieces. You'll have time to work on your secret project."

Juno stood and leaned over to peer at Taylor's laptop. "That's…impressive. Can I access any of that money now?"

Taylor nodded. "You can withdraw whatever you want and put it in the bank. Takes three to five business days to get there, though."

"That's incredible," Matteo muttered. "I didn't realize it was so easy."

"Well, it's easy because Juno has a following of people who know them and want to help out. It can be a lot harder for randoms to raise funds unless they're doing it for a really sympathetic cause," Taylor explained. "Because I know Juno and I'm familiar with their work and their following, I knew it would work and work fast."

Juno smoothed a palm over the back of Taylor's hand and lifted it to their lips. "Thank you, Taylor. If I had a child of my own, I'd want him to be just like you."

Taylor laughed. "You'd need more money than you're getting."

"True. Charles is quite enough for now." Juno moved back to sit beside his boyfriend, looking much more cheerful.

Vincent returned to the room, holding his phone up in triumph.

"We have a venue!"

"You're kidding," I said, hardly believing that things could work out so fast.

"Well, they did have a booking, but Tina, the agent, called the person who'd booked and asked if they could move their event to the following weekend if she offered a discount. I was doubtful but, according to Tina, they said they didn't mind."

"You do have a way with people." I placed my hands on each side of his face and leaned in to kiss him, then stared into his eyes for an emotional moment.

"Ew," Taylor commented. "Can we get the kissing out of the way so we can work on switching everything over to the new locale? This is going to take some major logistics wrangling."

"I can call people if you give me a list," Matteo said.

"So can I," I said. "Matteo and I will handle it. The rest of you, enjoy your evening."

I turned to Vincent. "But no more wine for Juno, please. They've been cut off."

Juno lifted their chin and huffed in indignation. But the look they gave me before I turned to leave the room held a touch of gratitude.

Chapter Ten

Since neither Vincent nor Charles had ever acted as human furniture before, Juno and I decided to have a practice session in a private setting, before we set them up as sushi tables at the main event. Matteo was also on board with this idea.

"Shall I serve our supper on them?"

"That might be overwhelming and impractical," I said. "But I appreciate your enthusiasm. I was thinking more of setting the two of them up as a coffee table in the living room for an hour. See how they manage."

"Ah, I see. Sounds divine." Matteo smiled.

I cocked my head. "Have you done any of that, Matteo? Objectification in the form of human furniture?"

"It's something I've experienced, yes."

"So we have an understudy? Excellent."

"Alas, my knees are getting a little bad for that sort of thing these days."

"Ah. But at the event you would be laid out on a table, on your back."

Matteo grinned and blushed in the most charming way. "I feel the younger men will look much better on display, honestly. But I can sub in in a pinch."

I put a hand on his shoulder and leaned in to kiss him. "Good to know. Don't undersell yourself, Matteo. Your body is divine."

"I'm glad you think so, Sir."

The following Friday evening, a week before the event, we put our plan into execution.

Vincent and Charles spoke together in whispers while Juno and I discussed the best way to proceed. It occurred to me to take them into the 'dungeon' for a short session to help them get into the submissive mind frame they'd need for this to work. When I told Juno about my idea, they expressed confusion.

Their kohl-lined eyes narrowed. "What do you mean?"

"I won't touch Charles, and you can watch. I just need to get them into a submissive mind set. It will be easier for Vincent to get into subspace in a familiar environment. I expect Charles will respond to the formal nature of the basement space as well. Have you seen the new bondage bed?"

"No, I— Bondage bed, you say?"

"I had it custom made."

"Well then, we should go downstairs. Charles, you heard Nic. Down you go. Vincent, too."

"Matteo, while we're downstairs, can you and Taylor move the existing coffee table out of the way and tidy up a bit?"

"Of course."

We'd let Taylor know what would be going on, and I'd expected him to fuck off to Riley's, but he'd said he'd help. At this point he seemed impossible to shock, and as long as Vincent and I weren't going to be having sex in the living room, he could handle it.

The kid was full of surprises.

"And maybe put some snacks in bowls or on plates. We'll want to use our human coffee tables for practical purposes."

"Yes, of course."

Juno and I herded the young folk down the basement stairs.

"Oh my goodness. That is quite the piece of furniture." Juno walked over to the imposing wooden frame that sported eye-hooks in every conceivable spot.

"We haven't actually used it yet—and won't be using it today."

Juno touched the smooth, varnished wood of the thick post at one corner. "That seems a waste. You should rent it out."

I snorted. "After having Daphne take over this space for a month, I'm averse to having anyone but me use it."

"Understandable.

"All right, you two. Strip. Everything off," I said, turning my attention to Charles and Vincent.

"Everything?" Charles asked, looking to Juno for confirmation.

Juno smiled. "It's up to you, sweetheart. You may keep your briefs on if you like, but you will be naked at the event."

Charles sighed. "I might as well take them off, then."

We waited while they removed their clothes and folded them with care. Charles didn't have the muscle definition that Vincent maintained with regular exercise and some minimal weightlifting, but he was just as attractive in a different way—gangly, like a young giraffe, whereas Vincent was lean like an antelope.

Charles stood awkwardly until he saw Vincent put his hands behind his head. He mirrored Vincent's pose, glancing at me for approval.

"Very good. Now, I would like you both to go to your hands and knees and crawl to my feet," I said, smiling and clasping my hands in front of me.

Charles watched with interest as Vincent obeyed, moving in the fluid, elegant manner he had perfected. Charles attempted to mimic Vincent's graceful movements without much success. He blushed in the most adorable way and, by the time he reached me, was in a similar state of excitement, which pleased me.

"Good. Now crouch down, press one cheek against the floor and hold that position."

Vincent obeyed with haste, followed by Charles. This wasn't anything new for Vincent. I liked to remind him of his subservient position in the playroom, and he thrived on this kind of objectification and mild debasement.

"Wonderful." I turned to Juno. "Do you mind passing me the crop hanging on the wall beside you? The brown one."

"Not at all," Juno said as Charles made a small noise.

"Do you ever use anything like this on him?"

"Oh yes, I have several. Even one that's glow-in-the-dark. We play around a bit," Juno said. They handed me the implement, then regarded Vincent and Charles with obvious approval. "They do make a nice pair. I'd like to paint them together someday."

I let my fingers slide along the leather of the crop. "Do you mind if I use this to tease them?"

"Please do. Nothing too intense, though. Charles is very sensitive."

"Noted. So is Vincent, although he can take a lot when he's sufficiently motivated." I tickled the tip of the crop at the small of Vincent's back, then ran it up to his shoulder blades, tapping between them. Vincent grunted, closing his eyes.

"What do you say?"

"Thank you, Sir."

I repeated the action on Charles.

"Thank you, Sir," Charles whispered — an obedient boy.

I returned the crop to Vincent, stroking him with the soft leather tip, moving it in lazy circles along his back and over his buttocks, then snapping it on each cheek. It made a satisfying thwack each time and elicited pleasing noises.

I repeated these actions on Charles, who made a charming squeal.

"Oh my," I said, grinning. "He *is* sensitive."

"Mm-m," Juno commented. "You should hear him when he—" Juno began to say. But Charles stiffened and Juno smiled. "Never mind."

I laughed and winked at Juno. "It's okay, I have a good imagination."

The crop had the desired effect, encouraging both men to focus on the tantalizing sensations of the supple leather on their skin and ground themselves in the present moment.

"All right. Up on your knees, please, with your hands clasped behind your necks."

Again, Vincent obeyed me with his effortless grace and Charles tried his best. He managed to get into the proper position, but I sensed it was taking a great deal to force himself into such a vulnerable position in front of someone like me, with a crop in hand.

"It's all right, Charles," I said, throwing him a kind smile. "I know you're a baby-sub, so I'll be gentle with you. You may close your eyes if it makes it easier. What's your safeword?"

Charles swallowed, his body flushed and on alert, his dick hard and chest rising and falling. He was into it but nervous and scared.

He glanced at Juno, who nodded.

"P—puppy," Charles stuttered.

I gestured silently to Juno, indicating his boy's tumescence.

Juno smirked and rolled his eyes, as if Charles' thorough arousal was to be expected. Charles gave off similar vibes to Vincent. Juno was lucky to have found him and seemed to have been clever enough to keep him, even after trying to drive him away.

I snaked the tip of the crop up the inside of Vincent's thighs as he flashed me a cheeky glance. I raised my eyebrows and smirked. He lifted his chin subtly as I tickled the crop over his testicles and drew it along the underside of his arching erection.

"Beautiful, Vincent. As always," I said.

"Thank you, Sir."

"Eyes down," I reminded him, and he obeyed in an instant.

I teased his cock with the tip of the crop until it became difficult for him to keep still, then I turned my attention to Charles.

Charles' eyes snapped open when he felt the tip of the crop on the inside of his knee, but he closed them again as I drew the implement up along the sensitive flesh there. I rested the fold of soft leather at the top of his inner thigh before running it under his balls to the other side.

As Charles let out a subdued moan, Juno and I exchanged a look.

It was titillating to have a new submissive in the playroom. Charles was a sweet, sexy man, and I imagined, in other circumstances, bringing him into our bedroom for an evening of fun and games. I didn't know if Juno would ever permit me that luxury, but it was entertaining to consider.

I drew the crop down to Charles' knee again then back along the same trail several times. He made wonderful sounds of supplication, his cock jerking against his stomach each time I tickled the leather fold under his balls. I hesitated, glancing at Juno, who watched with much interest. I raised my brows, and he gave a nod.

I traced the crop up the underside of Charles' straining penis.

"Oh! Oh! Oh!" he gasped and stiffened, his jerking cock shooting bursts of semen like a popped bottle of bubbly.

Vincent uttered a sympathetic whine, his gaze flashing to mine with a desperate intensity.

I pointed the crop at him and gave him what I considered to be a silent threat of instant death if he allowed himself to climax. "Don't you dare."

He swallowed, closing his eyes and maintaining control somehow. I wasn't having both of them orgasm off the cuff during a practice session. Charles, with his lack of experience and obvious sense of overwhelm, could be excused.

Juno, who didn't understand the issue, laughed and clapped their hands in glee. "Bravo, Charles. Exquisite."

"I do apologize, Charles," I said. "I had no idea that would happen."

Charles panted, trying to recover himself. "I'm not — I don't usually play with other people. It was a lot."

I put the crop down and approached, going to my knees before him, careful to avoid the wet spot on the floor.

"It's quite all right. It was lovely to watch. I'm sorry I pushed your limits."

Charles gazed at me out of his flushed, glowing face. "I'm sorry I made a mess."

I shook my head at him. "Juno, you have a sweet soul here. I hope you know that."

Juno smiled. "I love to see you like this, Charles. You are beautiful, honest and unpolished, and I love you dearly."

Charles blinked. "Really?"

"Of course I do, you silly boy," Juno murmured, coming around and taking my place as I stood and gave them room. "I've been in love with you for ages."

"I love you, too. Since we met, I've adored you." Juno took Charles into an embrace as they kneeled together on the floor of my dungeon.

I crooked a finger at Vincent, who rose soundlessly and came to me like a well-trained animal.

I kissed him on the cheek. "Let's go upstairs."

"Yes, Sir."

Taylor was sitting on the sofa holding a beer. He lifted it as we emerged from the basement.

"Cheers. How's it hanging?" he said, then observed his cousin's tumescent state. "Oh. Never mind."

Matteo took one look at Vincent and smiled warmly, gathering him close. "You look luscious, as always."

Vincent curled into Matteo's side and nuzzled the older man's neck, as Matteo stroked his naked arm.

"Taylor."

"Nic."

"Will you be observing, then?"

Taylor grinned. "Just waiting for a place to put my beer."

I rolled my eyes. "Thought you didn't like seeing your cousin naked."

Taylor shrugged. "Well, I've seen so many guys naked in Daphne's dungeon, it doesn't faze me. I might as well learn a thing or two. Besides," he said, leaning forward, "Riley has expressed an interest in some…kink exploration." He sat back, looking smug. "Obviously, I am not opposed."

I sighed. "I suppose it was inevitable."

"Probably."

It occurred to me that Taylor would be a natural Dom, and I wondered if Riley was at all prepared for what he was getting himself into. Then again, I had no idea what they did together. Maybe it was a done deal. Was it weird that this thought made me proud? *Huh*.

Juno and Charles emerged from the basement. Taylor sat up straighter when he saw Charles walking naked across the room.

"Charles. My man."

Charles blushed and smiled at Taylor. "Hi."

"How are things?" Taylor asked.

"Oh, you know. Same old, same old." Charles gave Taylor a bashful grin.

Taylor laughed and took a swig of beer. I observed the way his gaze caressed Charles' naked body. Riley and Charles were similar in build and stature, and I realized that Taylor had a type. But could I blame him?

I held out my hand to Vincent. "Come with me, gorgeous. Let's get you two set up."

I had the two men get on all fours in front of the sofa, side by side. Vincent's arms and legs were longer than Charles', so our 'table's' surface was somewhat uneven, but it would do. I thought about covering their mouths with electrical tape but decided against it, although Vincent would have loved that. They wouldn't be gagged at the event. Perhaps it was a good idea to rehearse how to ask for assistance in the case of an emergency. In deference to decorum, they faced the sofa, although I told them to keep their eyes on the floor.

Juno, Taylor and I sat on the sofa and chatted about different things while Vincent and Charles got used to the position. They did well, with only the occasional twitch.

After about ten minutes, I placed a large serving bowl of potato chips on each of their backs, near their shoulders, so we could reach them.

"I'm starting to see the appeal," Juno said, crossing one leg over the other and regarding their boyfriend's vulnerable predicament. They grasped a chip and took a bite, watching as a crumb fell into Charles' hair. "Oh, I'm so sorry," they said and reached to remove it.

I put my hand up. "No, no. Charles is merely a piece of furniture right now, Juno. He has no emotions or sensibilities that require an apology."

I reached for a chip and pretended to fumble it, dropping the whole thing on Vincent's head.

"Oh darn, I dropped one. I'll get another."

"You, Sir, are delightfully wicked," Juno commented.

"Oh yes, I know," I said.

"This is going to be quite the education for my darling Charles."

After thirty minutes had passed, signs that the activity was taking its toll began to emerge. Vincent showed the stress with minute movements of his muscles and small twitches of his splayed fingers. Charles, on the other hand, broke out of position in ways that became more obvious as the time went on, almost causing his bowl of chips to fall.

"Charles…be still."

"Yes, Sir," he said, forcing his body into stillness, even though it must have been very difficult.

"That's better. Not much longer. You're over half done."

He made a little noise. "I didn't know it would be this hard."

"Lots of things that seem quite simple are, in fact, very difficult," I said, petting him on the head in a departure from the scene. "Quiet now. If you need to safeword, do it. But see if you can last another twenty minutes."

"Yes, Sir."

Juno clicked his tongue. "My poor boy. He lives the life of luxury. He's not used to slumming it."

"You must have experimented with bondage?" I said, looking over Charles and imagining him in soft ropes.

"Oh yes. But I only ever use silk scarves."

I scoffed. "You're kidding, right?"

Juno narrowed an icy gaze at me. "You do you. I'll do me. And, best of all, I'll do Charles, the way I like to do Charles, and you can fuck right off." They took another chip, deliberately brushing crumbs onto Vincent's smooth back.

"Touché," I said, "But, really, that's not fair." I reached for a chip and broke it into pieces that landed on Charles.

"Now, now," Juno said, picking up the pieces of chip and tossing them to the ground. "No need to get petty."

I swiped the crumbs off Vincent and sat back, chewing contentedly. "They do look very nice."

"I can agree with you on that point," Juno said.

I decided to let them up early, because it looked like Charles wasn't going to make it. All-in-all, though, they'd done very well.

"Careful when you stand. You might be lightheaded," I said as Juno and I helped Charles and Vincent to get up. They looked flushed and alert, with sparkling eyes, as if they'd recently ended an intense yoga session.

"Why don't I go upstairs and run the bath? There's room for both of you, if it's all right with Juno," I said.

"Hmm. Can I trust Vincent to keep his hands off Charles?"

"I don't have a problem taking a bath with Charles, and yes, I can keep my hands to myself. You know I'm not a huge slut, right?" Vincent said to Juno.

"I'm so sorry. All I've been hearing from Nic is how much of a slut you *are*, Vincent. And I mean that in entirely a flattering way. I think all boys should be sluts, at least in their twenties. I certainly was — back when I was a 'boy'."

Charles gazed, fascinated, at Juno. "Really, Juno?"

"But of course I was. I highly recommend it. Although I'd prefer you to only be slutty with me."

I took Vincent and Charles upstairs while Matteo and Taylor entertained Juno. We had moved the real coffee table back into place, and Matteo had said something about tea. I kissed Vincent and gave a salute to Charles.

"Soak as long as you'd like. You did very well down there."

Once I got back to the living room, Juno was engaged in a discussion with Matteo of abstract art. The teapot had been brought out and teacups distributed. I poured myself some tea and listened.

"So, what makes one painting art and another one not art?" Matteo asked.

"Well, that is the tricky question. As long as a work is created by a human being, with the intention of expressing some kind of feeling or idea, it is considered art."

"So it doesn't matter how long an individual spends on a particular piece or project, it automatically becomes art when they create something?"

"Yes. Of course, that doesn't mean it is *good* art."

"Well…yes. That's the thing. Who gets to decide if something is good or not?"

"That, I'm afraid, is a question that hasn't really been answered yet," Juno commented, sipping from their glass of sparkling water. "It could be the market, but we know lots of art that is now considered to be good was not valued highly when it was created. Like Picasso, for instance. People thought he was mad."

"Bipolar, I thought," I said, sitting down and grabbing a chip out of the bowl that had been returned to the wooden coffee table.

"Sometimes a dash of mental illness can add to the creativity, don't you know."

I laughed. "I wouldn't have guessed."

Chapter Eleven

Daphne had gone out with Alexander a number of times, and I knew their relationship was progressing well. I couldn't believe Daphne had found someone who could tolerate all her quirks and peculiarities, but Alexander seemed to thrive off her unstable energy. I think it turned him on, that she was a whirlwind of adventure and experience.

From what Daphne had said the last time we'd spoken, they had resumed the Dom/sub dynamic that they'd had when Alexander had been Daphne's client, except that now he wasn't paying her — at least, not directly and not with money. He'd lavished her with material things, and it seemed she was enjoying that part of the relationship. I couldn't blame her. She was living her best life, and I was happy for her.

But I didn't expect her to call me up three days before our gallery event and tell me they were getting married.

"*What?*" I shouted into the empty house. Taylor was with Riley, and Matteo and Vincent had gone to pay a quick visit to Juno and Charles. I was tired from an intense day at work, so I'd begged off. I'd been sitting with my feet on the coffee table, but after hearing what Daphne had said, I sat up and planted them firmly on the floor. "Repeat, please. What are you saying?"

"Alexander and I are getting married. Aren't you happy for me, Nic?" Daphne was breathless with excitement.

"Well, I—um… I guess?" Her announcement had caught me off guard. They'd only been officially together for a couple of months. "It seems a little quick?" I ran my fingers through my hair and decided it was long overdue for a cut.

"Yes, I know. It is quick, I admit that. But, Nic, he's perfect for me. And I'm perfect for him. We fit, you know? Like you and Vincent and Matteo."

I laughed. "But *we're* not married."

Daphne hesitated. "Would you marry them if you could?"

Wow, that was not a question I thought I'd be answering tonight. When I considered what Daphne was asking, I had to give her an honest answer.

"I don't know."

"You don't know?"

"Daphne, it doesn't have anything to do with how I feel about them. It has to do with how I feel about the whole idea of marriage."

"Oh, I see."

"Because of the person I am, I don't want to be trapped in a role I'm not comfortable with. What's wrong with fully committing to someone without getting married?"

"Nothing. Nothing at all," Daphne said. "But I think I want to marry Alexander."

I thought about it and tried not to let my own feelings about marriage affect my answer.

"Daphne, I'm really happy for you. If you think Alexander's the one for you, that's fantastic."

She sighed with relief. "Thank you."

"I'm content with the way things are between me and Vincent and Matteo. I don't feel like we need a ceremony to prove our feelings for each other. To be honest, we've never discussed it, since a legal marriage between the three of us is out of the question," I said, rubbing my forehead. "You've given me a lot to think about. Anyway, when's the big day for you and Alexander?"

"We're planning a small ceremony and reception in the spring...probably May, maybe June. We're still working out the details. It won't be a traditional wedding."

"You don't say?" I laughed. "I'm thrilled for you, Daf. Really."

"Do you think Sparky would be our flower boy slash ring bearer?"

"I think he'd be delighted."

"Oh, Nic, I can't believe my life right now. I feel like Cinderella or some fucking thing. I don't even know." She laughed.

It was fantastic to see her so happy.

"Well, you definitely sound like you're in love. Congratulations."

She squealed. "Thank you! Can you have Vincent and Matteo call me when they get home so I can tell them? Don't ruin the surprise."

Well, I didn't ruin it. All I told them was that Daphne had an announcement.

I think Vincent thought she was pregnant. His eyes got big as saucers, and he opened his mouth to ask.

"Not that. Holy Christ, Vincent. Daphne with a baby? Can you picture it?"

He smiled and shrugged. "You never know."

"Anyway, just call her — before you guess and ruin her surprise."

I heard them talking to her on speaker phone and lots of laughter and congratulations. Afterward they told me she'd spoken to Taylor, and he had agreed to be her flower boy.

As we got ready for bed that night, stripping to what we normally wore beneath the sheets — nothing for Vincent, boxer briefs for Matteo and a T-shirt for me — I cleared my throat and opened a can of worms.

"Um, crazy question for you guys. Marriage. What do we think about it?" I pretended it was merely a philosophical inquiry.

Vincent stared at me. "Um, what?"

Matteo stared at me thoughtfully. "Marriage can be…complicated."

I nodded. "Yeah. I have a lot of not-so-great associations with it, like gender roles and societal expectations." I crossed my arms. "I don't think it's an option for me."

"That doesn't mean it isn't right for Daphne and Alexander," Matteo said diplomatically.

"Oh, I know," I said. "I'm happy for her. I hope it works out."

Vincent regarded me curiously. I wondered what he was thinking.

"Vincent, my love," I said, moving closer and taking his face in my hands. "You know I love you, even though marriage is off the table? Especially since we can't include Matteo?"

He smiled slowly, blinking in sedate contemplation. "But I could have worn the most beautiful white lacy underthings under my tuxedo."

I gasped. "Oh holy fuck," I said, imagining it. "That might have made me change my mind before Matteo joined us."

Matteo held up a hand. "If the two of you want to get married, I have no objections."

We swiveled to gape at him. "What?" I said.

"Matteo..." Vincent began.

"If you wanted to make things official between the two of you..."

"No," I said immediately. "I don't need society's approval of what Vincent and I feel for each other and for you, Matteo."

"I know that, but there are legal things to consider," Matteo said, propping himself on an elbow. "We've never talked about that."

I shrugged. "We'll get a lawyer, and draw up some papers to define our arrangement. We can do that, right?" I said to Matteo.

"I think so. Wills, powers of attorney and all that formality."

Vincent nodded. "Yes. We have Taylor to think of."

"True," I said. "We don't need a marriage contract, but maybe a legal will is a good idea."

"I know someone who could help us with that," Matteo said. "I'll call him this week."

I got into bed and Vincent gathered me to him, kissing me with an open mouth and eager tongue. Matteo crowded the two of us and joined in.

"You're *such* a romantic," Vincent teased when we broke apart, as he traced my cheek with a finger.

"Hey, I'm romantic," I said. "I'm going to romance your cock right now."

I grinned, kissing my way down his body.

"I pride myself on being unconventional, you see."

When I got down there, I pressed a kiss to the tip of his swelling penis and tickled it with my tongue. Then I climbed over him to get to Matteo and rubbed a hand down the length of the semi in his boxer briefs. I took the waistband and tugged it down, tucking it beneath his balls, and glanced up to see Vincent lean over and capture Matteo's lips with his own.

I grinned and marveled at the gifts an unconventional life could bestow.

* * * *

Since we'd had to switch venues and because the church had stone walls that we weren't allowed to mar, Juno displayed their works in random places — leaned against the walls, sitting in the window ledges, or propped up on tables. Although perturbed not to have a traditional way of mounting the pieces, once the pieces were scattered around the venue in seemingly random ways, Juno determined the look worked and made the paintings more unique and accessible. Guests would feel as if they'd stumbled into an artist's garret.

Vincent, Matteo and I picked up Charles and got to the church early, so that Vincent and Charles could prepare for their 'performance'. We had the maintenance person jack up the heat, so those wearing little could be comfortable. Matteo and I arranged the two tables, placed a layer of foam on top of each one and covered them with fancy white cloths, before putting Vincent and Charles into place. They lay still with their arms beside them and their legs straight, completely naked and blindfolded, with their cocks caged. I know Vincent was relieved to not have to worry about a raging erection over the course of the event, and I think Charles appreciated the wisdom of wearing the confining accessory.

Whether either one of them would find the experience arousing at all was up for debate. Their submissive hearts would enjoy it, regardless. They seemed nervous but I expected that would lessen as the time went on. Once we had laid out the sushi, I stood back to admire the esoteric beauty of it.

"I have to take some photos of this. Hold on." I grabbed my phone and snapped a dozen photos from every angle. "Stupendous."

"Sir," Vincent murmured.

"Yes, my darling?" I said, leaning in so he could speak in my ear.

"When will they start letting people in?"

"Soon. We're going to open the doors in a moment. Are you all right?"

"Yes. I just don't want to be lying here forever."

"Of course." I touched his arm. "We'll get started."

"Thank you."

Juno had arrived, resplendent in a peacock blue gown with metallic accents. They twirled to show it off, revealing black heeled boots.

"How do I look?"

"Like a bonafide eccentric artiste," I assured them. "Can you make sure Charles is comfortable? We're going to start letting people in soon."

Juno swished over to Charles and whispered in his ear. Charles' lips moved and Juno straightened. "He's ready to go…and so am I."

We had arranged for classical music to play over the sound system while our guests mingled and sampled the sushi. The entire setting was a contrast between stark and opulent, cold and warm, dark and light – the rough stone walls of the church versus the peaceful music and the silky texture of sashimi, the haphazard displays of artwork and the meticulously arranged limbs of our sushi models, the warmth of the tones in Juno's paintings versus the cooler accents of the decor and architecture.

Our guests seemed to appreciate the beauty and magic of the ambience. I checked in with Vincent and Charles often and devoured my share of delicious sushi off their artfully arranged bodies. The patrons grew accustomed to the unusual furniture in no time, although some were hesitant at first. The displayed men received many compliments as well as bold inquiries about the state of their genitals. At a regular buffet, we would have covered their bits with fig leaves or something similar, but since this was a kinky art show, we had decided to leave them be, making sure that all the food was placed at a respectable distance. Matteo and I kept a close eye to make sure none of the guests fondled the human tables inappropriately.

Charles and Vincent relaxed into their passive roles without much trouble. Although confident of Vincent's abilities, I had been curious to see if Charles would be able to manage his self-consciousness well enough to stay still for as long as required. In the end, they proved the perfect decoration for the event.

Once the hour was up and the crowd around them had dissipated, Matteo and I moved the remaining sushi to a traditional table and helped Vincent and Charles.

"So?" I asked, as Vincent sat up and I removed his blindfold.

He blinked in the ambient lighting. "That was…kind of fantastic. I'm floating."

"Excellent. Stay in that space. I'm taking you to one of the demo stations."

"Which one?"

"The shibari one. Easy-peasy…but still nice."

"Yes," he agreed. "What about Charles?"

I glanced to where Matteo was assisting Charles.

"I can ask him. I was going to let him get dressed, honestly."

"Let me ask him," Vincent said. He padded over to where Charles stood gazing about him at the well-dressed people wandering around, trying to come out of his submissive trance. Vincent gave him a gentle hug, which made Charles blush. Then Vincent spoke softly to Charles and Charles nodded, then glanced to me and asked another question. Vincent responded, then took Charles by the hand and led him over.

"How are you doing, Charles?" I asked.

"Fine. Good. I feel good."

"It wasn't too much?"

He shook his head. "It was easier than I expected."

"I'm glad. You looked delicious — both of you — covered in sashimi and sushi. I got lots of pictures."

"Vincent said you're taking him to the shibari demo. I'd like to participate, as well, if that's okay?"

"You want to get tied up like a pretty gift?"

"Sure. Why not?"

I grinned. "All right. Matteo, would you please take Charles and Vincent over to the shibari demo? Drake is expecting Vincent, but let him know that Charles wants to be involved, too. I'm going to find Juno and ask if they're okay with it and see how the art sales are going."

"Of course. Come along," Matteo said, leading the two of them to where Drake stood gathering up the rope from a previous demonstration.

I left Charles with Vincent and Matteo, and headed into the crowd to locate Juno. It wasn't difficult to find them. Not only because, true to form, they had dressed spectacularly for the event, but also because there was a gathering of people around them as they moved from art piece to art piece, speaking to the design and the emotions behind each work.

Daphne caught my eye and rubbed her thumb and index finger together, and when Juno saw me looking, they smiled wide and winked. I waited a few moments until they began to move my way then signaled that I needed to speak to them. They politely detached themselves from the group and approached me.

"Is Charles all right?"

"Yes, he's fine. I'm having Drake rig Vincent up in some rope. Charles volunteered to join him, but I wanted to check with you first."

"I'm not his keeper. If he wants to do it, it's fine with me."

"All right. I thought I'd check."

"Well, thank you." They went to move away, then hesitated and turned back. "Take lots of photos."

I grinned. "Most definitely."

By the time I got back to Drake, he was speaking to Vincent and Charles and gesturing with his hands and the rope. They nodded and laughed.

I was so glad we had been able to involve Drake in this event. His shibari skills were outstanding, and he was a genuinely kind and interesting person.

"Hey, Drake."

"Nic! Great to see you!" He pulled me into a hug. "I see I have two stunning subjects to work with."

"Yes. I'm expecting something extraordinary."

"Sure, sure. I'll see what I can come up with. Why don't you go mingle and have a drink while I get started. Check back in about twenty minutes."

"Sounds good. Are you two all right without me staying? Drake is a professional and a friend."

"It's fine," Vincent said. "Do some browsing. We could use another of Juno's pieces."

"Good idea. Come on, Matteo. Let's have a look around."

While Drake worked on his rope design with Vincent and Charles, Matteo and I grabbed drinks and walked arm-in-arm, speaking to guests and watching some of the demos. I had to admit, the event was going even better than I'd expected.

Cheese, crackers and bite-sized desserts had been brought out for guests to nibble on as they browsed. There were a variety of outfits, ranging from black-tie and cocktail dresses, to jeans and T-shirts, and some people were in kinkier leather ensembles. I loved seeing such a variety of individuals in such distinctive clothes.

We found a painting that we could afford and bought it for the dining room. So every time Juno came to dinner with Charles, they could see what we thought of their talent.

I ran into some I knew and spoke to many I didn't. I made sure to ask everyone if they'd had a chance to look at the artwork on sale, or whether they were interested in any of the demos. By the time twenty minutes had passed, Matteo and I wandered back to Drake's spot. A group in front of us broke apart, and I grabbed Matteo's arm.

"Matteo. Look."

"Dear God."

We gaped at Drake's handiwork, unable to move as we took in the erotic display before us.

Vincent crouched on his knees on a soft red blanket, his legs together, his back straight as he faced the floor, making a kind of table with his torso and head. His arms were stretched out behind him, hands clutching Charles' shoulders

Charles was splayed over top, his straight back against Vincent's, with his body inclined and his head downward, almost touching the floor. His legs were bent at the knee and parted so he lay over Vincent's shoulders, Vincent's head poking between them as he gazed at the far wall. They were knotted together with black rope in key places to help them maintain the pose.

Charles looked like a sacrifice, his belly exposed and his legs splayed, while Vincent supported him from below — a human pedestal. Charles held onto Vincent's shoulders, his wrists bound, as they made an erotic scalene triangle — a geometrical masterpiece of muscle and flesh. Drake had blindfolded them with black silk scarves, and they looked like a religious sacrifice.

Drake stood next to them with his hands clasped at his back, standing guard over his vulnerable subjects.

"Wow, Drake," I said as we moved forward. "That is incredible."

"Beautiful," Matteo agreed, his gaze fixated on the two young men. "Astonishing."

"Thank you so much," Drake said, smiling. "They are a joy to work with."

"How long can they stay like that?" I asked, noticing the straining muscles of Vincent's arms.

"I'm going to give them ten minutes. I don't want them to get too uncomfortable." He regarded them with an assessing gaze. "If they're up for it, we can do another pose afterward—one that's more natural and easier to handle."

I took out my phone and snapped a series of photos as I walked around the living sculpture. Vincent and Charles appeared frozen in time. Drake had put Charles, the smaller man, on top of my sleekly muscled, larger submissive.

As I watched, Charles' lips parted, and he sighed in serene supplication.

Matteo and I remained while Drake untied them. He left their blindfolds on and asked if they'd be willing to do another pose. Both men agreed.

This time, Drake had them kneel facing each other with their wrists bound behind their backs, chests roped together and their heads resting on the other's shoulder in a display of camaraderie and support. It delighted me to see them arranged in such an intimate way, and I hoped the experience would cause a deepening of the friendship already blooming between them.

Chapter Twelve

The event wrapped up at midnight.

Juno had made a total of twelve sales, adding up to a payout of almost fifteen thousand dollars. They were ecstatic and felt validated as an artist once again. I was so happy for them.

Taylor and Riley had shown up, dressed fancier than I'd ever seen them. Riley looked adorable in an aubergine suit that emphasized and enhanced his slight stature. Taylor wore a traditional black tux. They made a quick round of the fetish demos, and I showed them the photos of Vincent and Charles as sushi platters then shibari subjects. Taylor seemed impressed and not all that squigged out. He was getting used to his cousin's extra-curricular interests, and they didn't seem to bother him anymore.

Although Daphne and Alexander hadn't been able to attend, I called her with the news of our success.

"That's fantastic! I knew it would be a smashing event. I told everyone about it."

"I know. I think you were responsible for about a third of the attendees. Your name came up a lot."

She giggled. "Well, you know, I do have quite a reputation in this community."

"Yes, you do. Thank you, Daphne. We appreciate it."

"Hey, of course! By the way, is Sparky going to be around tomorrow?"

"I'll ask him." I turned to Taylor. "Daphne wants to know if you're going to be home tomorrow."

"Here," he said, holding out his hand. I put the phone in it.

"Daf? What's up?" He took Riley's hand and led him to a spot where he could speak somewhat privately.

"Charles, my sweet, I couldn't have done it without you," Juno said, kissing their boyfriend. Charles and Vincent had dressed but still seemed buzzed and euphoric from their experiences. "And from what I've heard and seen in Nic's fantastic photos, you were the absolute stars of the event! Did you enjoy it, darling?"

Charles wrapped his arms around Juno and nodded against their shoulder, glancing at me and Vincent with a smile.

"Well, that's good, because I feel the distinct need to get you into some ropes again, very soon. I've got Drake's business card."

Charles laughed.

"Oh, you think I'm joking," Juno commented, placing a hand on their hip.

Charles shook his head. "I'm not that stupid," he said, his voice muffled against Juno's shoulder. "But I don't mind. It was fun."

Juno gazed at Vincent. "And you... Thank you for taking such good care of him. As the more experienced one, I'm sure Charles benefited from your relaxed state of mind."

"Charles was the perfect partner," Vincent said. "I think we shored up each other."

"I'm quite certain our guests will never forget the sight of the two of you covered with expensive fish and seafood. I know I won't," I said. "My mouth waters remembering."

"Because the sushi was so good?" Vincent teased.

"Sure, we'll say that." I rolled my eyes.

Taylor returned and handed my phone back. "She wants to come over tomorrow afternoon to explain my flower-boy duties. I told her I will not crawl down the aisle but, other than that, I'd be willing to negotiate."

Riley laughed. "This should be interesting."

I raised my eyebrows. "Daphne is always interesting."

I pocketed my phone and gathered Vincent's and Matteo's hands in mine. "Let's go home."

* * * *

Back home, Matteo and I peeled off Vincent's clothes and sent him to the shower. When he returned to the bedroom, we confiscated his towel and worshipped him as he lay on our bed. He seemed astonished to be the center of so much attention.

"A little aroused after all the delicious visuals?" he said, arching his neck and stretching out to give us access where we needed it.

"You could say that," I remarked, trailing kisses up the inside of one thigh as Vincent gasped. I glanced at Matteo. "Do you want to fuck him before I take off the cage?"

Vincent whimpered but Matteo gave me a breathy confirmation. "Yes. I want to empty my balls into this beautiful boy."

I grinned, circling Vincent's slim ankles with my hands and tugging him flat, then crossing one over the other and flipping him onto his belly in one practiced move. He grunted and bounced on the mattress, then let out a harsh curse as Matteo grabbed his knees and forced them apart.

"Could you get me the spreader bar?" Matteo said.

Vincent made a startled sound and whipped his head around. When he saw Matteo's determined expression, he turned his face into the mattress and shuddered.

I located the spreader bar and passed it to Matteo, then settled back against the dresser to observe, saving my energy for later. Watching Matteo fuck Vincent, when Vincent was obviously desperate for it and prevented from a satisfying culmination by the device on his junk, was one of my purest pleasures. I also knew it satisfied Vincent to be used as a fuck toy for Matteo's enjoyment and filled with Matteo's spunk.

Matteo deftly fastened the cuffs of the spreader bar to Vincent's ankles, then hauled him up so he was on his knees. He stuffed a pillow under Vincent's chest for support.

"Fuck," Vincent muttered, realizing he was entirely at Matteo's mercy, and Matteo meant business. Normally sedate and sensible, when Matteo had been teased and tortured all evening with the sight of two gorgeous young men in minimal clothing and an environment of hedonistic, artistic appreciation, he became hyper-focused and relentless.

Still, Matteo hesitated as he examined Vincent's vulnerable rear as it presented itself for just about anything. He glanced my way.

"Did you want to spank him or anything?"

"Oh no, Matteo, be my guest. Do with him what you like." I was more than happy to watch.

Vincent turned his dark and desire-filled eyes my way as his mouth parted wantonly. I understood Matteo's driving need as a spike of pleasure shot through me.

I walked over to Vincent and stroked my fingers along his flushed cheek.

"Tell you what, my darling. You let Matteo have his way with you, and I'll take the cage off afterward so you can fuck me," I said, picking at a hangnail and pretending to be bored. "And if I'm pleased with you, I may even let you come."

"I think Matteo's going to have his way with me right now, regardless," Vincent panted.

Matteo slapped Vincent lightly on the butt cheek. "You can always safeword, you nincompoop."

"I know. But that seems like bad sportsmanship in this situation."

Vincent was clearly as turned on as we were after everything he'd been through tonight. I was eager to see my two favorite men getting it on, especially with Vincent immobilized as he waited for his imminent dicking.

Vincent squealed as Matteo dripped a steady stream of cold lube onto the small of his back that dribbled down between Vincent's cheeks and over the spots that needed to be slippery.

"Easy, boy," Matteo murmured as he spread the lube around and fingered Vincent in an efficient and emotionless way. "Just getting you ready."

Vincent groaned as Matteo's fingers invaded him, slipping inside his hole with intent and purpose. I moved back to my spot at the dresser for a better view.

"Nice," I commented. "He enjoys a good frigging."

"So do I," Matteo remarked, causing Vincent to squirm and grunt with his aggressive prep.

Because the cage over Vincent's cock prevented him from focusing his pleasure in that specific area, his entire body would become engaged in what Matteo was doing. The intensity would increase in so many ways, precisely because Vincent's attention wasn't focused on his penis.

Also, because he'd been caged almost twelve hours and subjected to so much frustration and titillation at the gallery show, his body was primed for pleasure wherever it could find it. And right now, it was finding it at Matteo's hands.

"Oh, fuck. Oh God," Vincent moaned as Matteo pumped him vigorously with two fingers. "Please, Matteo. Fuck me. You said you were going to fuck me."

"Patience, my love. You'll get fucked when I'm ready. I'm working up all the spunk I'm going to bury inside you."

"Jesus! Oh, God," Vincent groaned, arching his back and sticking his ass out for Matteo.

Matteo and I exchanged a glance. My expression must have betrayed my amusement at Matteo's filthy language, because he quirked his lips and shrugged.

"It's true," he said.

"I know. But I so rarely see this side of you, and I'm loving it."

Matteo took his cock and rubbed the crown against Vincent's buttock, then slapped him with it. "This is what you're getting, and everything in my balls when I shoot into you."

"Fuck," Vincent replied, turning to gaze at me with a desperate expression. "Help."

I shook my head from side-to-side. He could ask all he wanted, but unless he used his safeword, I wouldn't interfere.

"Quiet," Matteo directed. "Keep your ass in the air, Vincent. It's so pretty like that."

The hoarse sounds of Vincent's breathing filled the space as he became more and more frantic. Matteo's fingers trembled as he prepared himself with the lube and moved in from behind. When the head of his cock pressed against Vincent's hole, Vincent cried out, "Please!" through clenched teeth.

Matteo leaned forward and rubbed his clean fingers against Vincent's lips. "If you need something to do with your mouth, suck on these," he said. Vincent took Matteo's fingers in his mouth as Matteo's cock breached him.

Vincent groaned as Matteo sank into him from both ends.

"My God," Matteo groaned as he drove into Vincent's soft, warm hole, picking up speed as he became more and more excited. "You are so pretty from this angle."

Vincent garbled against Matteo's fingers as Matteo pounded him, his desperate sounds accompanied by the creaking of the bed and my hastened breathing.

I snuck a hand into my pants, rubbing myself as I watched them. They were so fucking hot like this. My gasps mingled with theirs as they moved together toward Matteo's culmination. I moaned as the orgasm took hold of me, but I kept my gaze on them as Matteo abandoned the last of his composure.

"Oh…God…Vincent," Matteo swore, pulling his fingers from Vincent's mouth in order to use both hands to grip as he thrust wildly, then froze as he emptied into Vincent, a euphoric look on his face. Vincent cursed and groaned as Matteo filled him, unable to chase his own satisfaction, but no doubt enjoying the degradation of his plight.

"So much. I gave you so much," Matteo said, withdrawing with care and watching his semen leak from Vincent's body.

"That is so fucking hot," I breathed, wiping my wet fingers on my pants and moving closer.

Matteo pushed his still-hard cock back into Vincent and Vincent whimpered as his hole became a plaything for me and Matteo. The next time Matteo's cock slipped out, I used my fingers to push the spunk back inside.

"Get one of the plugs and stuff that good stuff up there," I said, since Matteo's dick was softening, and I couldn't bear to waste any of it.

Vincent groaned again, thrusting his caged cock against the air as Matteo found one of our many butt plugs and brought it over. I twisted the tip at Vincent's slick hole and gently pushed it into him.

"There. All stoppered up."

"I can't take it. I need to come. Please!" Vincent begged, ragged with need and frantic with desire.

"Shh. Soon, my darling," I said.

We unbuckled him from the spreader and turned him over, and I retrieved the tiny key for the cage from my watch case. I held it up in Vincent's line of sight.

"Oh, thank God. *Please.*"

Our poor baby was so gone. He needed his dick back and he needed it now. And although my sadistic heart could have made him wait another day, or an entire week, his performance and the care with which he'd assisted Charles the past few weeks encouraged mercy.

Plus, I was so ready to get that cock of Vincent's inside me, especially knowing that he was full of Matteo's seed.

My velvet jacket was long gone. I stripped off my pants and unbuttoned the white shirt, then crawled onto the bed and put the tiny key into the lock on Vincent's cage. He sighed with relief as I slipped the device off and gave his cock the freedom to fill with blood. I handed the key and the cage to Matteo and bent to kiss and lick Vincent's poor, abused penis, until it stood at randy attention before me, and Vincent was barely able to keep quiet. One of his hands snaked down to touch himself but I clicked my tongue.

"Oh no you don't. This is mine now. Hands off. Matteo, cuff his wrists and attach them to the D-ring in the wall."

"Yes, Sir."

Vincent groaned in frustration but didn't resist as Matteo did what I'd asked.

"Now you're all mine, Vincent. I'm going to ride this cock until you can't control yourself. But if you come before I say you can, I'm going to get off before you finish, and you'll be spurting into the air like a broken water pipe." I turned to Matteo. "Get the rubber bit-gag. I want him quiet and at my mercy."

"Of course."

Matteo found the gag and brought it to me. Vincent watched him with adoring eyes and opened his mouth obediently so Matteo could place the thick cylindrical rubber bit between his teeth.

"That's it," I crooned, hovering over him. "Who's my good pony?"

Vincent closed his eyes and blushed bright red, moaning and squirming as if the very idea of it were enough to drive him mad.

"Oh, he liked that," Matteo said.

"Are you my good pony, Vincent? Would you like me to put a tail in your ass and trot you around the ring? I could bridle you and give you blinders and lead you into the street for the whole world to see."

Vincent's eyes flashed open, and he grunted, shaking his head back and forth.

Matteo and I laughed.

"Well, maybe in our own private paddock, then, out in the sun on a warm summer day? You could be a good pony for me then I could bring you home and take off all your tack and reward you, like I'm about to reward you right now."

Vincent gave a groan so pleading and desperate that I actually felt sorry for him. I took the lube from Matteo and gave Vincent's cock a good coating before positioning myself over the top of him and guiding it into my body.

I cursed as I sank down on Vincent's hot hardness, trying not to focus on the expression on Vincent's blissed-out face as he struggled to control himself. I took him all the way and then sat there, motionless, so I could acclimate to his invasion.

"Oh fuck, darling, you fill me up so perfectly."

Vincent, who was prevented from speaking by the bit in his mouth, flashed his blue eyes, the pupils so dark and dense that they appeared bottomless.

"Give me a nod when you're ready for me to move."

He stared at me with hooded eyes as he tried to slow his breathing and keep from coming too soon. After a minute, he inclined his chin and gave me the sign that he could take more. I slid my body over his, maintaining our connection as my mouth found a nipple, which I tongued aggressively, feeling his cock swell and shudder inside me.

"Argh!" Vincent moaned, his knees coming up behind me, shifting us and causing his cock to move inside me as he braced his feet on the bed.

I groaned and attacked the other nipple, licking and nipping the sensitive bud while Matteo watched from the sidelines.

"When I sit up, Matteo, you're going to come sit beside him, and take both of these nipples in your fingers, using a light pressure until I tell you to go hard. Got it?"

"Yes, Sir."

Vincent regarded Matteo with trepidation, knowing that this would challenge his control in a most excruciating way.

"Ready, baby?" I whispered. "Here we go. I won't make you wait long, but don't you dare go off before I say."

I sat up, bracing my palms on Vincent's thighs behind me, gripping him for balance, as Matteo moved in and took Vincent's nipples between his fingers.

"One," I said, sliding myself up and back down on Vincent.

"Two," I said, repeating the maneuver as Vincent's eyes did the same.

"Three."

I nodded to Matteo, who squeezed Vincent's nipples hard as I moved like a beast on Vincent's cock.

"Come when you can, darling," I panted, just as the orgasm took me. I couldn't hold back the sound that came from my throat as I clutched Vincent's thighs with white-knuckled fingers, the hot spike of his cock sending me over the edge and into a tumult of ecstasy.

Vincent arched off the bed and screamed behind the gag as he joined me. I met Matteo's open-mouthed gaze as Vincent bucked beneath me and filled me with his seed, the spunk from Matteo's earlier release lodged in his plugged passage.

Vincent screeched again then fell to grunting as my orgasm ebbed down to a milder hum and I slid off to attack his gagged mouth as Matteo released his nipples and moved aside.

As I peppered Vincent's slack face with grateful kisses, I shot out my hand and grabbed Matteo, bringing him in to us.

"I love you both. You know that, right? I can't even imagine what I'd do without you. I don't want to imagine it."

"Neither do I," Matteo murmured between kisses, while Vincent accepted our devotion with happy, sated sighs.

Chapter Thirteen

"Skating? You mean, on ice?" I said, biting my lip as I contemplated this fresh horror awaiting me.

"Zarah wants to meet us at the canal," Matteo replied.

"That sounds like fun," Vincent said, folding laundry and piling it onto the sofa.

Saturday had dawned sunny and cold, but the temperature would rise to just under freezing over the course of the day.

"You can skate, right?" Vincent said, glancing at me.

"Sure," I said. "I've done it once or twice."

I picked up a shirt from the laundry basket and concentrated on folding it.

In actual fact, I had skated a total of *two* times, and neither of those times had gone well. I sensed their gazes on me, and when I looked up, they were staring at the shirt in my hand.

"What?" I finished 'folding' it and placed it onto the pile of shirts that Vincent had done. It didn't look quite right.

While I watched, my sweet, submissive Vincent slowly picked up my contribution to his pile, shook it out and folded it properly.

I crossed my arms and pouted.

"Do you know how to skate, Nic?" Matteo asked.

"Hmm. Well, depends what that means, really," I grumbled.

Vincent glanced at me. "Can you move around on the ice and not fall too much?" he said.

"Vincent, since we are talking about ice, I'd like to suggest that you are on a very thin surface at the moment."

"You don't scare me," he said, flashing his baby blues. "And you can't skate, can you?"

I gave him a penetrating look, meant to reassert my dominance and assure him of my competency at whatever I chose to attempt. But then that seemed like too much work.

"Fuck," I said.

Matteo and Vincent exchanged a glance.

"I didn't think there was anything Nic couldn't do," Matteo said, with a smug look on his face.

I held up my hand. "There is nothing I can't do that I want to do. I don't *want* to go skating."

"Hmm," Matteo muttered. "The only thing is, I've already told Zarah we'd meet her at the canal around two this afternoon. She's eager to get out."

I cocked my head. "Is it even wise for a pregnant woman to skate?"

Matteo frowned. "She's not even showing yet."

"I don't know what that means."

Vincent was trying not to laugh, which I thought was extremely unfair. I pointed a finger at him.

"Stop. It's not an area I'm familiar with."

"Like skating?"

"Oh, fuck off."

Vincent huffed a laugh. "I'm sorry. It's simply cool to know you're not an expert in absolutely everything.

"Yes, well, pregnancy is definitely one, and skating is another. So, what are we going to do?" I said.

Matteo picked up the empty laundry basket and headed for the bedroom door. "We're going to meet Zarah at the canal, and if you want to keep your boots on, you can. Or you can 'man' up and rent some skates."

I glared at him. "That's a low blow, Matteo."

He shrugged. But he had a point.

"I'll fall. What if I break my leg?"

Matteo rolled his eyes. "You're not going to break your leg."

I put my hands on my hips. "How do you fucking know?"

"Because there will be three of us there to help you."

I scratched my chin, conflicted. On the one hand, I didn't really want to put on skates. On the other hand, what was the big deal? In all honesty, I was afraid of looking stupid.

"Can Zarah even skate?"

"Yes. It was her idea."

"Well fan-fuck-ing-tastic," I sighed. "Fine. I'll do this." I pointed at them one at a time. "But if either of you makes fun of me, laughs at me or tricks me into falling head-first into a snowbank, you will pay for it back here tonight."

They could barely suppress their amused smiles as I resigned myself to my fate.

* * * *

What did I get myself into?

I sat on a bench in the lobby of the Dow's Lake Pavilion, tying up my rental skates. It had been too long to contemplate since I'd attempted this questionable... sport? Pastime? I wouldn't be here now except to show my support for Zarah and Matteo, which was an important thing to do.

Vincent and I had accepted that Zarah and her forthcoming child were going to be a vital part of Matteo's life, now that she'd left her asshole of a husband. Far be it from me to stand between a parent, their child and future grandchild. I would support Matteo in whatever he decided was important, as long as it didn't compromise our relationship.

So I did up my borrowed hockey skates and tried to stand. Vincent and Matteo, who had already laced theirs and now watched me as I struggled, didn't offer assistance. I had scared them off with my bad-tempered silence in the car, since I was insecure about being out of my comfort zone and likely to get mad. But now that I had the damned skates on, I was worried about injuring myself.

"Can I get some help here?" I asked, clutching the arm of the chair I was trying to lift myself from.

They each took an arm as I managed to stand on legs that wobbled in an alarming manner.

"Where did you say we were meeting Zarah?"

"The Bronson rest area," Matteo replied.

I blinked at him. "And where's that, exactly?"

"On the other side of the lake," Vincent replied.

"The other side of the— I don't suppose we could have agreed to meet her at a charming canal-side café, instead?"

Vincent and Matteo kept me from falling as I chicken-walked over the carpeted floor to the doors that led out to the ice. I was too preoccupied to appreciate in full the way my partners were dressed, in thick sweaters, jeans and jaunty toques—a traditional outfit on the Rideau canal in Ottawa for temperatures above minus ten. I was thankful for the moderate weather, since it had been bitterly cold the week previous, which meant the frozen canal had been maintained and was in good shape for skating. Now that the sun was well on its way across the sky, the full warmth from its rays became evident, which meant I couldn't complain about the cold, only about everything else.

"Sorry. When I agreed to this, I assumed you could skate," Matteo said. "I should have made sure."

"It's fine. I'll be fine," I said, determined not to be a whiny little child. "Just help me get to the ice."

I tried to ignore the highly entertained glances Vincent and Matteo kept exchanging, that they didn't think I saw. At least *they* were having a good time.

I remembered the mechanics of skating, but the execution was lacking in many, many ways. I kept my arms out to either side like a five-year-old and did as well as I could.

"There you go!" Vincent encouraged as I slipped precariously forward.

Matteo frowned at his watch.

"What?" I demanded.

"I told Zarah we'd meet her at two, and it's ten after."

"Oh fuck. That's my fault," I said. "Go on. Let her know we'll be there as soon as we can."

Matteo looked at me, then at Vincent. "Are you sure?"

"Yes!" I said. "Go."

"All right. Thanks," he said, peeling away from us with the skating skills of an NHL hopeful.

"What the *fuck*?" I said. "How can *he* skate so well?" I glared at Vincent. "Can *you* skate like that?"

"Like what?" Vincent said benignly.

"Like…expert level. *Can* you?"

Vincent shrugged. "I don't know what you mean."

I closed my eyes, clutching his arm. "Are you a good skater? Tell me the truth, or I will cage your cock for a month."

"Nic, you don't scare me."

"Yeah, I do. I'm the Big Bad Dom."

"You only scare me if I want you to."

"Vincent, you are ruining the only thing I have to cling to right now."

He grinned. He wasn't sorry at all.

"Can you skate well?" I asked again with succinctness.

"Sure. Yeah."

"Are you better than Matteo?" I gestured to Matteo, who was already a small figure in the distance.

"I don't know," Vincent said, giving me a smug smile. "Look… I grew up skating. It was what we did as kids, all the time." He eyed me. "What did you do as a kid? In the winter, I mean."

I blinked. That was a long time ago. "Played the piano. Read books. Gazed out of the window at the neighborhood kids lugging their skates to the rink."

Vincent looked shocked. "What? That's so sad."

"I was obsessed with my music back then. I'm starting to realize I may have short-changed myself." I looked down at my skates as I attempted to orient myself as we moved forward. "And, uh, I didn't get along well with most kids my age."

Vincent was quiet. Then he said, "That must have been tough."

I shrugged. "It wasn't their fault. I didn't fit into any of the neat little packages their parents had told them about. I wasn't much of a girl. At that time, I wasn't much of a boy, either. I was an awkward loner with a music habit." I grinned at him. "A skinny little runt."

He snorted. "Yeah, right!"

"I was…ugly and not very likeable. At least, by high school, I could pull off the heroin chic look with my stringy hair and bony cheekbones."

"Huh. I can't picture it," Vincent said, keeping me steady. We were about halfway there, now.

"Count yourself lucky. I didn't keep any photos from those days."

We continued on without speaking. Then Vincent said, "How did you finally, you know…figure yourself out? Your identity and all that?"

"Bowie."

"Pardon?"

"David Bowie. I was obsessed with him as a musician, and he was the first androgynous, gender-fluid person I'd ever seen. When my dad died, I inherited his record collection. Makes me wonder if maybe my dad wasn't a bit gender-fluid himself, even though I never saw an outward sign to indicate that."

I had felt an instant connection to Bowie's lyrics and had had a visceral response to his pose on the cover of *Hunky Dory*, where he reclined on an antique chaise in a medieval-type dress, sporting voluminous, curly locks. It had awakened something dormant, or at the very least undefined, inside of me. If Bowie could dress like that in public—on the cover of a record album—maybe I could dress the way I wanted. Maybe I could live my truth.

"Wow," Vincent said.

"Bowie didn't give a fuck what other people thought. And after that, neither did I."

Vincent met my gaze. "You are the bravest person I know."

"Oh, come on. I don't feel brave right now," I said. But my mood was starting to lighten. Dow's Lake was crowded with people who were laughing and joking and having a good time. It was difficult to keep myself separate, and maybe it was time to stop trying.

"Once I gave up attempting to conform, everything went in a masculine direction. One of my girlfriends started calling me 'Nic' and, it felt right. Eventually, I asked her to refer to me as 'him', and she never questioned it."

"Wow. That's pretty amazing."

"Yes, it was. Daphne was always ahead of her time."

Vincent laughed. "How long have you known each other?"

"I think we met in fifth grade. Well, I was in fifth grade. She was older. I remember her using curse words and knowing all sorts of very interesting sexual things. She fascinated me."

"She fascinates me *now*."

"Yeah. I can't believe she's getting married. It just seems so bizarre. I never expected Daphne to want to get married."

"Sometimes people surprise you."

"Like Matteo and Zarah," I said, peering ahead at the rest stop filled with picnic tables and bordered by a Beavertails shack and a changing station.

We were almost there, thank goodness. I located Matteo and Zarah, standing side-by-side near one of the tables. Even though they were bundled up, and Zarah's dark complexion had absorbed a good amount of her mother's Nigerian blood, it wasn't difficult to see the resemblance.

"There they are," Vincent said. "Do you want to try to skate on your own, or are you happy to keep holding on to me?"

I clutched Vincent tighter. "Don't let me go!"

"Never!" he said, laughing. "I've got you."

When we finally made it, I could tell Matteo was trying not to laugh at me.

"Fuck you," I said, then turned to Zarah. "I do apologize, but he's being an ass."

Zarah grinned. "Yes, a bit. I don't think it's very nice to laugh at people who are doing their best."

I gestured to Zarah, glaring at Matteo. "Oh, I like her."

"I'm sorry," Matteo said. "Can I buy you a coffee as an apology?"

"Yes! All will be forgiven if you do. And a Beavertail, please. Killaloe Sunrise."

"Anyone else?"

Matteo took orders and skated to the short lineup at the refreshment shack with Vincent, leaving me perched on the bench of the picnic table with Zarah. It was a relief to be off my skates. I stretched my legs out and leaned back on my elbows, gazing up at the blue sky, listening to the scrape of blades and the sounds of laughter and conversations.

"You're not a skater," Zarah said with a smile.

I turned to face her. "Not really, no. I don't do sports."

"Matteo tells me you're a musician. A teacher."

I glanced at her, appreciating her warm eyes, broad mouth and rosy cheeks in a way I hadn't appreciated another woman in a long time. She was literally stunning.

"Yeah, although I don't play much anymore." I frowned. "Which is a shame, really."

"I'd love it if you'd play something on the piano for me the next time I come over."

I smiled. "Sure."

"Nic, I wanted to apologize for suddenly appearing out of nowhere. I understand why Matteo didn't tell you and Vincent about me, although he probably should have." She looked into the distance. "My husband is a piece of work."

"I heard. In that case, I'm glad you left him. And it's been nice to find out more about Matteo's past."

Zarah smiled again. "I'm sorry I suggested the canal. I haven't been skating in a long time and won't be able to in a few months, so…"

I held up my hand. "It's fine. It's been very amusing for Vincent and Matteo to see me off my game. They live for these moments."

Zarah laughed. "Your game? What do you mean?"

I waved my gloved hand in the air. "Oh, I like to pretend I know how to do just about everything." I gave her a frank look. "They enjoy my confidence but find it hilarious when I'm out of my element."

"They think very highly of you."

"We think highly of each other."

Zarah nodded. "I'm glad my father has a family. I haven't been much of a family to him," she said, frowning.

I didn't know what to say, so remained silent and looked at my skates and the sunlight glinting off their blades.

"I should have left Dennis long ago. I shouldn't have taken him at his word…ever."

"That's a difficult thing to learn, sometimes, for an open, trusting person."

"Yes, it is. I've wasted so much time. He was very restrictive. Leaving him wasn't an impulse decision, you know. There was no marriage left by the time I found out I was pregnant. It was time. You know, I gave up all my friends for him — as well as my father, although I didn't realize I was being lied to. I was lucky to have friends who were pleased to hear from me and helped me when I asked, even though they hadn't heard from me for a very long time."

"Good friends will stand by you."

She nodded, watching Matteo and Vincent horsing around in line. Vincent had picked up a handful of snow and shoved it against Matteo's neck. They struggled, laughing, as Matteo tried to get him back.

"And fathers. Even when you break their hearts," she said.

I reached out and put my gloved hand on her arm. She covered it with her own. For Matteo to pretend that his only daughter had never existed showed how much he'd been hurt. But it hadn't been Zarah's fault, in the end.

"You're so young, Zarah. Matteo is nothing if not loyal…and protective of those he loves. He would kill for you."

Zarah swallowed. "I know he would. He won't need to."

"You don't think Dennis will do anything stupid? Now that you've left him?"

Zarah looked exhausted all of a sudden. "I don't think he cares that much, now that I'm gone." She gave me a somber look. "Even if he found out about the baby, I don't think he'd care. In fact, he wouldn't want the trouble of it."

"I'm so sorry."

She shrugged. "No, it's better this way. I want a new life. I don't want anything to hold me back."

I returned my gaze to Vincent and Matteo. Vincent looked in our direction. I gave him a thumbs up. He smiled and turned back to Matteo, whispering in his ear.

"Oh fuck, they're conspiring." I gestured to them, and Zarah laughed.

"You are lovely together...all of you."

"We're a lot to take on."

"No, you're not." Zarah touched her belly over the wool coat she wore. "I'm so glad to be getting to know you. And at least Dennis gave me something of value."

"You're much braver than I would be in the same circumstances."

"Thank you. That means a great deal, because you seem very brave."

I laughed, tucking my skates under the bench and sitting up straighter, gazing at her with raised eyebrows. "Because I came out to the canal, when I can't skate for shit?"

"Exactly."

We sat together in silence, soaking up the sunshine, until the others returned with our drinks and snacks.

"Getting to know each other?" Matteo asked as he passed Zarah her hot chocolate and gave me my coffee.

"Yep. Your daughter is delightful, Matteo. I'm glad she found her way back to you," I said, as Vincent passed Zarah her Beavertail.

"Careful, it's hot. And the lemon juice runs sometimes," he said.

"Oh, I know how to eat one of these. I remember." Zarah met Matteo's gaze. "Dad used to bring me here all the time."

Matteo smiled. "Yes, I did."

"Mom wasn't very outdoorsy. But as soon as the canal opened each year, Dad would take me skating. And we'd go as often as we could," she said, taking a bite of her sugary treat. "Does Taylor skate?"

"I think so," Vincent said.

"We should bring him next time," Zarah asserted.

"Yes, you should," I declared. "Because I don't think I'll be back."

They made noises of protest.

"Uh-uh. Next time we want to all get together, we can meet at a nice restaurant or a café," I asserted, "Or we'll have you over for supper, Zarah. You must remember your dad's skills in the kitchen."

"I do recall, and I can't wait to taste his spaghetti Bolognese again."

"I'll make it for you on Sunday, if you'd like," Matteo suggested.

"I'd love it, if it's okay with the others?"

"Of course. You're welcome anytime," I said.

I meant it. Zarah already felt like a part of the family.

Chapter Fourteen

For the past couple of months, because I'd been feeling the strain of always being in charge in the bedroom and basement, Vincent, Matteo and I explored being together without the frequent entertainment of formal BDSM scenes. And you know what? It hadn't been half bad.

There was no way we could be entirely vanilla, even in the short term. And although I no longer planned intricate scenes with my two lovers, the power dynamic came through in other ways—and something very interesting began to happen.

One afternoon, when we'd come up to the bedroom straight after work to get our horny on, I'd gone into the bathroom to freshen up. The door was ajar, and I hesitated for a moment and watched.

Vincent, on all fours in the middle of the bed, naked, with his shoulders down, his back arched and his ass out, presented a pretty picture of supplication. Matteo, in his boxer briefs, was worshipping that boy's ass. But what was more interesting were the whispered commands I could hear that made my sweet boy shudder and shake with anticipation while Matteo reduced him to a quivering husk.

Someone had been paying attention. *Someone* had a secret capacity for domination and control. *Someone* enjoyed debasing and humiliating Vincent just as much as I did.

It was a bit of a revelation, to be honest. Matteo had always been content to serve, whether in a domestic context or a sexual one. But it seemed that with me absent from the room and having let go the reins to our sexual dynamic, and after his experience at the play party, Matteo had found a new calling.

I stood at the cracked bathroom door, happy to observe them in silence. The fact that they didn't notice my absence was…freeing. All at once I didn't feel solely responsible for them, for their pleasure and satisfaction. I realized that Matteo and Vincent had as much of a bond with each other as I had with each of them and that it was okay to pull back. And sometimes, when that happened, other beautiful things bloomed to replace old habits and routines.

"Oh my God," Vincent moaned, spreading his legs as Matteo held his cheeks apart and went at his ass with a determined tongue. "Oh, fuck."

"Do you like that?" Matteo murmured, his mouth making obscene sounds as he licked and sucked at Vincent.

"Oh fuck, yes. *More.*"

Matteo chuckled. "Nic'll be back soon."

"No, no, no, no, no…" Vincent panted. "Don't stop."

"I won't," Matteo said, glancing my way.

He saw me standing there, relaxed, calm, observing. I was wearing a pair of snug blue boxer briefs and a singlet, with an unbuttoned navy shirt. Matteo's eyes widened and his lips, shiny with spit, parted.

I lifted my index finger to my mouth and nodded toward Vincent. I wanted Matteo to continue. I only wanted to observe.

Matteo gave an imperceptible nod in return, as Vincent whined and writhed, his hand snaking under his belly to grab hold of himself.

"No no," Matteo said, with the same tone he used to stop people from sampling a meal he'd made before it was ready. "Stop that."

He gave Vincent's ass a slap. The sound echoed off the walls and caused Vincent to yelp, then moan. Vincent brought his hand forward, crushing the bedclothes in his fist and rutting against the mattress.

"Should we stop? And wait for—" Vincent moaned.

He meant me. My good boy didn't want to get in trouble.

"No. It'll be fine," Matteo said, his voice rough. He picked up a tube of lube that lay nearby and opened it, coating his fingers with the slippery liquid.

I leaned against the bathroom counter where I could still see out of the door and shoved a hand down the front of my boxer-briefs, fingering myself while I watched them. This was better than porn—taking a back seat and watching what they did together. They were beautiful, and they were mine.

Vincent arched his back like a cat and just about purred he was so content. Matteo knew exactly what Vincent liked. He'd watched me, and he'd been paying attention. It was like seeing an apprentice come into his own when you hadn't even realized the talent was there.

Vincent would become suspicious if I didn't appear, so when Matteo slicked up a finger and inserted it into

Vincent's ass, I strode out of the bathroom and made my way to the desk beside the bed. Vincent's gaze flew to Matteo, but Matteo didn't stop what he was doing, so Vincent's startled gaze landed on me.

"Quiet," I said to him, pulling the straight chair out and arranging it to facilitate the view. "Since Matteo has you well in hand, I'm going to watch. You do look very pretty with Matteo's fingers in you up to the knuckle."

"Yes, Sir," Vincent moaned. "Thank you, Sir."

"I'm not the one you should be thanking," I said, leaning forward. "Who is the person owning you right now?"

"Matteo. Matteo," Vincent gasped, as the man in question fucked him hard with two fingers.

"So, thank Matteo."

"Thank you, Matteo. Thank you," Vincent panted, letting his head hang as Matteo worked his magic.

"It's my pleasure, Vincent."

When Vincent closed his eyes, I gestured to Matteo, my hand picking up a pretend remote control and aiming it at Vincent's rear. I raised my eyebrows.

Matteo smiled and nodded, giving our boy a couple of hard pumps with his fingers and then pulling them out and slapping Vincent on the ass again—hard.

"Three words," Matteo said. "*Remote. Control. Plug.*"

Vincent made a pitiful sound, because he knew where this was going.

"No…no, no, no."

I couldn't help smiling. Vincent had a love-hate relationship with the vibrating plug. It made him feel so good, but he found it extremely difficult to control his orgasm. And he knew that neither Matteo nor I would go easy on him.

"You have your safeword if you need it," I reminded him. "Tell me what it is."

Vincent sighed, turning his head to meet my gaze. "S-stitches."

"Now show me the hand that had the stitches."

Vincent lifted his left hand while Matteo found the vibrating prostate plug — Vincent's evil nemesis — in the drawer.

"That's right. And are you very careful when you use knives now?"

"Yes, Sir. *Very* careful."

"I know you are. And Matteo's taught you some good techniques, right?"

"Yes, Sir, he has."

I flashed Matteo a grin as he lubed the thick bulb of the prostate massaging plug, staring at Vincent's hole with an eagerness he couldn't conceal.

"I'm going to let Matteo control this, Vincent. Do you have any objections?"

Vincent stared at me, his blue eyes vulnerable and vast. "No, Sir."

"Good. I'm going to sit back and enjoy the show."

Matteo chuckled. "I'll do my best to please you, Sir," he said.

I waved him off. "Just have fun. Don't worry about me."

Matteo inclined his head.

Vincent shuddered and dropped to his elbows, spreading his knees. Matteo pressed the tip of the prostate massager against Vincent's hole and pressed steadily until it went in. I watched the emotions flit across Vincent's expressive face as the toy stretched him, then seated itself inside. He mewled his pleasure and dropped his forehead to the bed.

Matteo adjusted the prostate plug to ensure it was sitting properly, causing Vincent to yelp. Then he reached under Vincent's belly and gave his cock a few strokes, making it firm up even more than it was.

"You're lovely," Matteo sighed.

"Thank you," Vincent murmured, his shoulders and back muscles clenching in anticipation of what was coming.

"I'm turning it on. If you get close, let me know," Matteo murmured

"Yes, Sir. Thank you." Vincent side-eyed me with a smug look because I didn't always give him a break, even if he was struggling to hold back.

I shrugged. Matteo could play this any way he wanted to.

When the vibrations began, Vincent's forehead creased and his mouth opened. Anal stimulation had a huge effect on Vincent, so we always started at the lowest setting. But even giving a mild vibration, the toy caused Vincent to stutter and stammer as his hips rocked and his buttocks clenched.

"Steady," Matteo said, placing his hand on Vincent's lower back. "Accept it. Stop fighting."

Vincent visibly relaxed, taking a couple of deep breaths. Matteo tickled the skin at the top of his thigh. "You look gorgeously violated."

"Thank you," Vincent sighed.

It was fun to observe the two of them together. Perhaps that was what I'd needed all along — to give myself permission to step back and understand that Matteo and Vincent were capable of entertaining each other. Our sexual bond as a throuple didn't rest entirely on my head.

I crossed one leg over the other and settled in.

Matteo continued to fondle Vincent's cock while the prostate massager did its work. His forehead wrinkled in concentration as he knelt behind Vincent on the bed and used his fingers to touch and tickle him into a frenzy of frustrated arousal—a favorite pastime.

I loved watching Vincent struggle, because I knew that on some level he enjoyed every minute of it.

"Oh...fuck," he moaned. "Oh, please," he begged, arching his back and scrabbling his fists in the bedclothes. "Matteo. Matteo!"

"What's wrong?" Matteo said, and I had to give him props. He sounded confused and oblivious to Vincent's predicament, even as he played his fingers along the underside of Vincent's arching erection.

"Oh my God!" Vincent swung his gaze to me in desperation. "Sir! *Help*."

I raised my eyebrows, flicking an imaginary piece of lint from my pants. "Whatever for?" I said. "Matteo's doing a stellar job with you."

"Oh!" Vincent emitted a helpless groan and thrust against Matteo's touch.

Matteo and I exchanged an amused glance.

"Matteo, that reminds me. What are you planning for Thanksgiving? Are we doing a turkey and the whole shebang?"

"Oh, I hadn't really thought about it," Matteo said. "Although, I would like to invite Zarah."

"Yes, of course. The more the merrier. What about Daphne and Alexander? And Juno and Charles?"

We ignored Vincent's moans and grunts as we discussed trivial details.

"And Taylor and Riley. Good Lord, there will be a lot of us."

"We could always do a buffet supper. What do you think? A traditional menu?"

"Yes, I'll cook a large turkey—with all the standard sides, of course." He kept one hand on Vincent's straining cock and drifted the other to his tight testicles. "New potatoes," he said, cradling Vincent's balls in his hand, pushing and manipulating them as if he were considering how to prepare them. "And roasted vegetables." He drifted his fingers from Vincent's balls, over his taint, to shove absently at the prostate plug, making Vincent squeal. "And of course, stuffing. Lots and lots of savory stuffing."

With every syllable, he pushed at the prostate massager in Vincent's rear, causing Vincent to grunt and gasp.

"Close. *Close!*" Vincent gasped.

Matteo withdrew and picked up the remote, switching the toy off.

Vincent fought for control as we watched, his body tense, his head down in concentration. Clear fluid dripped down the side of his standing dick in tantalizing trails.

He rested his head on his hands and sighed, a sheen of sweat glistening on the back of his neck. "Fuuuuck."

"Close one?" I said.

"So close," Vincent confessed, rubbing his head against his forearm. "It's easier when my hands are restrained. I just want to jerk it. It's so hard to keep my hands off."

"Is that so?" I said, without an ounce of sympathy. "You're doing just fine."

"Yes, Sir," Vincent muttered.

Matteo repeated his actions, bringing Vincent close to the edge again and again, until Vincent's voice grew hoarse from the sounds he was making, and he struggled to keep from dropping to the mattress and rutting against it. But he was a good boy and didn't give in.

Finally, Matteo wrapped his fingers around Vincent's cock and jerked it relentlessly, causing Vincent to curse and yell as he came violently over Matteo's fist, shooting ropes of jizz onto the bedspread as I leaned forward to observe.

"Holy fuck, Vincent. That was epic."

Vincent groaned with exhaustion as he rode the aftershocks as his orgasm waned. Matteo wiggled the base of the still-vibrating plug.

"Oh, God," Vincent muttered, collapsing to the bed. "Turn it off. Turn it off."

"What's the magic word?" Matteo said with a mischievous smile.

"*Stitches.*"

Matteo turned off the vibrations and eased the plug out of Vincent's ass.

"I was going for 'please', but that works. Sorry."

"No, you're not," Vincent muttered. "Fuck you."

"He gets nasty after he gets what he wants," I commented.

"Fuck!" Vincent swore then glared at me. "What the hell?"

I raised my eyebrows.

He swallowed and licked his lips. "I mean, what the hell, *Sir*?"

I lifted my hands. "What?"

Then Vincent glanced at Matteo and arched like a cat before rolling onto his side, exhausted.

"Ooh, you are channeling kitty vibes right now, Vincent," I said.

"Hmph," Vincent muttered.

I glanced at Matteo, who smiled.

I clicked my tongue. "You want to be a grumpy kitty, fine. But you come over here and thank Matteo."

The naked planes of Vincent's back lifted as he sighed, but he pushed himself up and slid sinuously off the bed onto his knees, crawling to Matteo with exaggerated, cat-like movements. He met Matteo's gaze with seditious intent.

"Oh, hell," Matteo breathed, his hand pressed against his erection over the cotton of his boxers as his young conquest approached.

"Meow," Vincent mewled, licking his lips and nearing Matteo with his chest lowered to the floor. When he got close enough, he rubbed his forehead against Matteo's ankle.

"Good kitty," I said, pleased that Vincent was playing along.

"Meow," he said again, rubbing his cheek on Matteo's calf, sliding his hands up the outside of Matteo's legs. Soon, Vincent slid his fingers beneath the waistband of Matteo's boxer briefs and pulled them down, revealing Matteo's stiff cock, which bounced before him.

Matteo gasped, his eyes wide and fixed on Vincent.

"Very good, kitty. Now get Matteo to give you his yummy milk," I said.

Matteo groaned and circled the base of his cock with his fingers, rubbing its moist head on Vincent's cheek. Vincent turned and engulfed Matteo's erection between his lips.

Matteo's eyes rolled back in his head as Vincent got to work, whimpering and growling while he sucked and teased.

Matteo didn't last long. His breathing ramped up as he steadied Vincent's chin and thrust into his mouth, crying out as he came over Vincent's tongue and chin.

"Lap it up, little kitty," I encouraged as Vincent swiped at Matteo's release and swallowed what he could.

"Mmm-m. Meow!" he said enthusiastically.

I laughed, then knelt and kissed Vincent with affection, licking up what was left of Matteo's sweet spunk.

Matteo wiped himself with a wet cloth.

"Matteo, please take this kitty into the shower and give him a thorough rubdown. Clean his bits well because they are going on lockdown for at least a week."

"A *week?*" Vincent spluttered, throwing me a horrified look.

"You want to make it two?"

"No, Sir," he said. "Thank you, Sir."

"Good boy. Now get in the shower."

* * * *

Vincent lasted four days before he begged to be allowed to come.

"I did four loads of laundry, changed the bedsheets, vacuumed and mopped. I did everything."

Vincent had followed me upstairs after work and was trailing me around the room, trying to convince me he deserved a reprieve.

"Did you dust?"

"I dusted on Tuesday."

"So you didn't dust today?"

"Well, no. But I—"

"Then you didn't do *everything*, Vincent."

He looked crestfallen. "I'm *so* horny."

I shrugged. "I'll have Matteo milk you."

Vincent sighed. "But it hardly helps at all. It just reminds me of what I'm missing."

I stopped what I was doing and gave him a firm look. "You know, Vincent, this is very undignified behavior. If you need to use your safeword, do it."

Vincent frowned. "I don't want to use my safeword. I just want to come!"

I laughed. "I've never seen you behave like this, but I know just what to do about it."

"Oh no," Vincent said, backing away.

"Oh yes," I said. "Do you know what you're going to do?"

Vincent pressed his lips together and he looked like he wanted to argue, even though I hadn't said anything definitive yet. But the flush in his cheeks showed me he was also very, very curious.

"You're going to strap on one of the dildos, Vincent, and fuck either me or Matteo, or both of us, with it, while your poor little penis stays in its little cage."

Vincent blinked. "What?"

"You heard me."

"But…but…Sir."

I moved in close and cupped his chin in my hand. "That will teach you how to be of service without gaining any kind of reward for yourself. I should think that would be something very appealing to you."

Vincent opened his mouth to say something. I could see the wheels turning as he thought about what I'd said. He closed his mouth and gave a little sigh of forbearance. Then nodded sharply. "Fine."

"Oh, I wasn't asking."

Vincent trembled. "No, Sir."
"Good. Then we're on the same page."
"Yes, Sir."

Chapter Fifteen

The following afternoon, just after I'd gotten home from work, Taylor came in, stomping his feet and complaining about the cold.

"It's February." I looked him up and down. "Maybe if you dressed properly for the weather, you wouldn't get so cold." Then I contemplated what I'd said and sighed. "Jesus Christ. You've turned me into my mother." I sidelined him a glance. "I hope you're happy."

"Indubitably."

"Matteo's making stew for supper. That should warm you."

"Yes!" He fist-bumped the air and headed into the living room.

Taylor greeted Vincent and plopped down beside him.

"Hey," Vincent said, not looking up from the book he was reading.

Taylor side-eyed his cousin.

"What's your problem? You're more sulky than usual."

Vincent held up his book and gave Taylor a cold look. "Reading. See? A book. With pages."

"Oh God. Is this some kind of discipline-gone-wrong, thing? I don't even want to know." Taylor lifted his hands in surrender. "I'll go help Matteo with dinner."

I took his spot on the sofa next to my pouty boy.

"You know, Vincent, for someone who responds well to teasing and denial, I'm finding your reaction to be quite puzzling."

Vincent shifted on the sofa and winced. He remained silent.

"Is it really that bad?" I asked.

He shrugged. "I've been thinking about using my safeword."

"Really?"

"Yeah. But I think if I do, I'll regret it."

"Vincent, we can stop whenever you want. I'm not legitimately trying to torture you."

He raised his eyebrows at me.

"Okay, fine. But only if it's good for you." I ran my fingers through his short hair and kissed him on the cheek. "Would it help if I remind you how sexy I find it that you're wearing that cage because I've told you to, and that you are relying on me for any sexual pleasure you might be permitted to receive?" I nibbled the shell of his ear.

Vincent whimpered. "Yes."

"That helps?"

"Yes...more."

I laughed, puffing hot breath onto his wet lobe. He shivered.

"You are so hot when you submit to me and my evil wishes. I love to tease you past the point of sanity, my darling."

"Is that what's going to happen tomorrow?"

"You bet your bottom, baby."

"Okay. Will I get to come after?"

"After what?"

"You know, after I do what you're going to make me do."

"Which is?"

Vincent glanced toward the hall. "I don't want to say it. Taylor might hear."

"Then whisper in my ear."

"Fine." Vincent put his mouth to my ear. "After I fuck you with the strap-on."

"And Matteo."

"*And* Matteo."

I grinned, pulling away and biting my lower lip in anticipation. I nodded.

The way Vincent's eyes lit up was comical.

"If you do a good job of it—and please us and don't complain, I will let you come."

"Really? You're not tricking me?"

"I'm not tricking you. I promise to let you come tomorrow if you fuck us both senseless with the dildo."

"Okay."

"So, you'll perk up? And be cheerful?"

"Yeah. As long as I have that to look forward to."

I laced my fingers with his and pulled him to a stand. "You are a very good boy," I said, kissing him, my hand rubbing over the metal of the cock cage under his clothes. "I don't deserve you."

"That is absolutely true," he said, removing my hand and twisting away from me. "Let's go see if dinner's ready."

* * * *

While we ate, Taylor regaled us with stories of Riley's new kitten.

"Seriously, this thing is so cute. I may have been replaced, actually." Taylor frowned.

"Doubtful," Matteo commented. "But kittens are nice."

"Maybe we could get one?" Taylor said.

"Negative," I stated, helping myself to more mashed potatoes.

"Nic, come on."

"I already have a kitty," I said, sidelining a glance to Vincent.

"What? Oh, come on." Taylor turned to Vincent. "Seriously?"

Vincent fought a smile. "Meow?"

"Fuck you guys." Taylor turned to Matteo. "Please, can I get a kitten? I promise I'll look after it, and you won't have to do anything."

Matteo smiled. "I'm afraid I'm with Nic on this one. We have a very lovely kitty already that doesn't need a litter box…or flea treatments."

Taylor scooped more potatoes onto his plate. "Fine. But I don't think it's fair."

I winked at Vincent. "I'm sure Vincent would pretend to be a kitty for you, Taylor, if you asked him."

"No thanks. No offense, Vincent."

"No worries," Vincent said.

"It's not all about sex, you know, Taylor," I said, cutting my pork chop.

"Really?" He said, glaring at me. "Why do I not believe you?"

"Vincent enjoys pet play in a non-sexual way, too."

"Wow, what a relief," Taylor muttered.

"Can we stop talking about cats? Please?" Vincent protested.

I tickled him under the chin. "But you make such a pretty pussy."

We ate in silence.

Then Matteo said, "Anyway, I'm allergic to cats."

I put down my fork and pinned Matteo with a glance. "You could have just said that at the beginning."

* * * *

The following evening, I attached my favorite dildo to the leather harness and buckled it around Vincent's hips, pulling the straps nice and snug. "Isn't this a great invention?"

"I used to think so," he said, gazing down at the long, silicone shlong that wasn't his own.

"Oh, buck up. You still have all the control."

"Very funny."

"I mean that you can take your time or get us off quick. Whatever you want."

"Who first?" Vincent said.

"Hmm…Matteo. Because watching you fuck Matteo with that thing will prime me nicely."

As scenarios went, it proved satisfying for everyone except Vincent. After he'd coaxed an intense orgasm from Matteo, and several from me, he had to lie down and take a break. He was coated with sweat, his damp hair plastered to his forehead, and a dark flush colored his pale skin.

I placed a kiss on his knee, and he groaned. "I'm so fucking horny. I won't survive this."

I exchanged a glance with Matteo.

"You should have had Vincent do that," I said, pointing to the cloth Matteo was using to clean up.

"The poor man's suffered enough, Nic, don't you think?"

"Fine. Okay." I was too blitzed on serotonin to argue.

I walked over to the dresser and retrieved the tiny key. Matteo crawled over and hovered above Vincent, stroking his skin and kissing his neck and shoulder, while poor Vincent whimpered and squirmed. Matteo played with the cage on Vincent's captive cock, cupping it in his hand and jiggling it up and down.

He gave me space so I could unlock the device. Vincent gasped as I slid the cage off his dick. I tossed the device, dripping with Vincent's pre-ejaculate, onto a nearby towel.

"You're so wet, baby," I murmured, fisting his slippery cock and coaxing it to hardness in a matter of seconds.

"Oh God, oh God, oh God!" Vincent muttered, hoisting up on his elbows to see what I was doing. I took him in my mouth, slurping eagerly and using my tongue to tease him.

Vincent's head jerked back, and his lips parted on a gasp as he stared at the ceiling.

"May I have a taste?" Matteo asked, moving close.

"Of course."

I aimed Vincent's dick at him, and Matteo got busy on it.

We took turns, until Vincent couldn't stand it anymore.

I had Matteo hold Vincent down while I aimed Vincent's cock at my open mouth and jerked it hard and fast. He came on a strangled scream, his body twisting and jerking as he painted my tongue.

* * * *

I was getting my groove back, and they would suffer for it. I surprised them with another scene a few days later.

Now that I'd had time to contemplate a number of scenarios, it was time to use our new bondage bed. I had come up with an ingenious way to break in this particular piece of kinky furniture.

To begin, I had them strip, kneel at the foot of the bed and wait for me. I didn't specify how long I'd be. This entire exercise would be a game of stretching their patience very, very thin.

I was pleased to see them in position when I got down there. Matteo seemed to be in a state of patient serenity, but Vincent looked fidgety.

I didn't speak as I fastened cock rings around their bits and walked around collecting the things I would need. I had to remind Vincent to keep his eyes on the floor a couple of times as I put them both in leather collars and wrist cuffs. Matteo's collar was thicker and forced his chin up. Called a posture collar, its design made it impossible for the subject to look down.

"All right, Vincent. Up on the bed. All fours."

Vincent seemed relieved to change position and for the softness of the mattress to replace the hard floor. I blindfolded him, then buckled his wrists together at the small of his back so he had to support himself on his chest, with his ass raised up. Then I attached his collar to a D-ring on the headboard. It held him in place, so he couldn't move backward at all. This element was intrinsic to the exquisite torture I was about to inflict.

I had Matteo kneel behind Vincent, with his cuffs attached to a D-ring in the bed frame above him. The posture collar meant that he couldn't look at Vincent — only at the wall behind the bed. But I'm sure he remembered how Vincent had looked, and that image was going to torture him for the next little while, as he hung there, unable to take advantage of Vincent's vulnerability.

Matteo's erection bumped against Vincent's ass as I placed a ball gag between his lips. "Mmm-hmm. Are you starting to see where I'm going with this?"

"Mmm-hmm," he murmured, his gaze fixed on the wall.

Vincent cursed. He could feel the slick head of Matteo's cock slide against the skin of his hip. So close, but not in the spot he wanted it. He couldn't back himself any closer.

"Oh, I almost forgot," I said. I went upstairs and got the large ice pack from the freezer. It was a foot square. When I got back to the basement, I slipped it onto the bed, directly under Vincent's belly and his arching cock.

"I've put an ice pack right underneath you, Vincent, just in case you get any ideas about changing your position."

Vincent gasped, as if he couldn't believe the depths of my depravity.

"Have fun, guys. I'm leaving you here for an hour."

I placed a round bell into Matteo's palm.

"I'll leave the door open, so if either of you needs to safeword, I'll hear you. Oh, wait."

I brought over a bottle of lube and proceeded to grease Vincent's hole, making as much noise as I could, so Matteo would understand what I was doing.

"I'm just getting him ready for you, Matteo. All slicked up and shiny and desperate. If only you could figure out how to get your dick into him."

Vincent groaned as I stretched and probed him, while Matteo made hopeless noises and pulled on his restraints.

"Here... I'll even lube up your cock, Matteo," I said, doing just that, while he tried to avoid me and whined with frustration.

I smoothed some lube over Matteo's erection and left to dry my hands. I returned to check their positions, making sure they were near enough to touch, just not close enough to converge. I had to congratulate myself on the ingenious piece of predicament bondage.

Matteo's cock arched against his belly and bumped into Vincent's ass whenever Matteo shifted.

"Have fun," I said, slapping Matteo on the backside and withdrawing to the sounds of heavy breathing and a frustrated curse from Vincent.

I went upstairs and into the kitchen to make a sandwich. Best to get my mind off what was going on or I'd have to go get myself off. As I often did when I found it difficult to leave my men alone for the time required, I called Daphne.

"Hey, Nic. What's up?"

I laughed. "Oh, two very frustrated penises, at the moment."

"Do tell!"

I described the basement bondage scenario.

"Oh, that's so evil. I love it!"

"I haven't heard anything from down there, so I assume they're okay with it."

"How long are you leaving them like that?"

"An hour. Then I'll go in and see if they want me to lend a hand."

Daphne laughed. "I'm sure they will."

"So, how are things with you?"

"Oh Nic. Am-az-ing!"

"Good! Plans for the wedding going well?"

"Yes! It's as if this were always meant to be."

"Aww, man, I'm so happy for you, Daf. You deserve someone who gets you, y'know?"

"Thank you. I never thought I'd find anyone that…tolerant." She laughed. "Look… You'd better go check on your captives. I wouldn't worry too much about Vincent, but Matteo's not a young man."

I frowned. "He's only a little older than me, Daphne. In fact, he's your age?"

"Well, you're not getting any younger."

"Goodbye, Daphne."

"See ya."

"See ya."

I hung up the call and put my phone on the table. Then I sat there, delaying the pleasure of checking in on my tormented captives. Finally, when I couldn't stand it anymore, I walked to the basement stairs and started down. I stopped a few steps from the bottom. From this vantage point, I could see everything.

Matteo's skin shone with sweat, and his thigh muscles quivered with effort as he tried to push his cock closer to its target. It slid and glided ineffectually over the surface of Vincent's plump ass, leaving both of them in a state of frustrated agony.

The futile grunts and whimpers, the creaks of the bed frame as Matteo tried and tried to get enough friction on his cock, and the rub of the leather cuffs on their hook thrilled my sadistic heart—and fueled the raging fire in my blood.

I slid my hand into my jeans, touching myself while I watched this magnificent display of desperation and desire. I watched them with hooded eyes as my breathing ramped up. My climax hit—a quaking, violent thing that broke over me while I tried not to make a sound. Once my breathing steadied, I stood, wiped my fingers on my jeans, and made my presence known.

"Having fun, boys?" I said, ambling up to the bed and leaning against the thick post where Matteo could see me for a moment before the discomfort of the collar forced his eyes away.

Vincent, who was not gagged, made desperate pleas on their behalf. "Please, please, please. Sir! Please!"

I clicked my tongue, ignoring him. "Vincent's hole is so wet and ready for you, Matteo. But fucking someone is tricky when you don't have a pair of hands available to help, isn't it?"

Matteo groaned and Vincent cursed me.

"Did you want some help?"

Matteo made a strangled sound and jerked against his cuffs, making the bed creak.

"Oh, come on, Sir. Nic. *Please*," Vincent begged as he tried to look around at me, his eyes wide and frantic. Matteo thrust helplessly into the air.

This was going to be interesting.

"I should lube you guys up a bit more. The other stuff has probably dried by now." I opened the bottle. "Don't you dare come, either of you, or this game is finished. And whoever goes off early won't get a chance at another orgasm for days."

Vincent stayed still as I stroked a thick clump of grease onto his hole, spreading it around with my fingers and preparing him for Matteo. But he couldn't help the whimpers and groans that escaped him, now that he was getting some of the friction he was after.

Matteo closed his eyes and tried to keep his hips still, his cock like steel in my hand. He stuttered harsh breaths as I greased him up and tried not to rut against my fingers.

When that was done, I moved forward and unclipped Vincent's collar from the bed. He almost sobbed with gratitude.

"Here, move back a little, until your thighs touch Matteo's."

I helped him, as Matteo began to thrust in haphazard movements. He was all animal instinct now, like a stallion that had been led to a mare.

"All right, now." I guided the head of Matteo's dick to Vincent's slippery hole.

"Brace your knees, Vincent, and let him in."

I held Matteo's cock steady as he pushed it into Vincent's welcoming orifice, as both men groaned at the exquisite contact. Matteo shoved and fucked Vincent as well as he could, but his cock popped out and slid against Vincent's buttock a few seconds later.

He whimpered with frustration while I guided him back into place. Every time Matteo tried to get a rhythm going, his cock would slide out on the back thrust.

The next time I put him back in, Matteo made the most of two shallow thrusts, and as his cock escaped its lodging once again, streams of milky spunk arched in the air, landing on Vincent's lower back as Matteo cried out with relief and achievement.

A sob escaped Vincent's throat as Matteo's release splattered his skin.

I pushed three fingers into Vincent as I wrapped my hand around his cock and jerked him with rough strokes. He thrust into my hand, clenched around my fingers and came with a cry.

It took two hours, a hot bath, and several glasses of wine before they'd deign to speak to me. But when they did it was with a begrudging respect and an admission that, although tortuous and sadistic, the scene had been a resounding success. I looked forward to devising even more ingenious ways of torturing them.

Chapter Sixteen

Juno wanted to surprise Charles with a special gift. They still suffered residual guilt for their behavior during their mini-breakdown, and their therapist had suggested they try to make amends.

"Are we just supposed to pick out any puppy?" Vincent asked, on the way to the breeder in Stittsville. I rode shotgun, and Matteo sat in the back seat. Both of my men had insisted on helping to select the perfect puppy for Charles, and who could blame them?

"Oh no. Juno gave me strict instructions. It has to be healthy and alert—"

"Obviously," Vincent said.

"But they want a black and silver puppy, if there is one. When they spoke to the breeder on Thursday, there were three left with that coloring—one male and two females. They don't care what gender it is, of course, but it needs to be—and I quote—'a fitting addition to our aesthetic.'"

Matteo put a hand to his forehead, then chuckled. "The idea of finicky Juno bringing a dog into their swanky apartment is…unexpected."

"I know. But the breed is reasonably small and non-shedding. They do tend to be yappy, though," I said.

We exchanged a glance.

"Like Juno?" Matteo said mildly.

"Hold your tongue," I said, but couldn't help smiling.

"Wouldn't it have made more sense to let Charles pick out the puppy?" Vincent asked. "It's going to be his, after all."

"Juno wants it to be a surprise."

The breeder's house was on the outskirts of Stittsville proper and tricky to locate. Thank God for Google Maps. When we parked in the driveway and got out, a number of handsome little dogs ran to the backyard fence and began a jovial round of barking.

"That keeps the burglars away," I said.

Matteo smiled. "Yes, it would."

Vincent walked right up to the fence and held out his hand to be sniffed and licked with much frenzied affection. He glanced back at us.

"I don't know how aggressive these dogs would be with a burglar — probably lick him to death." He turned back to the group of dogs fighting to get to him, wagging their stub tails. "Okay, I admit, they *are* cute."

I raised my hands. "We're here for a puppy for *Charles.*"

"Actually?" Vincent said with a surprised smile. "I was hoping that was a set-up and you were secretly planning on letting me pick one out for *us*"

We made our way to the front door as I digested that bit of information. I glanced at Matteo, who raised his eyebrows, as if he'd thought the same thing.

"Are you kidding? You're kidding, right?" I said.

"I wouldn't be opposed to bringing a pup home," Matteo confessed.

"But...you're allergic!"

"To cats. Not to dogs."

"Oh fuck, I don't know. Do we really need a dog? Do we *want* a dog? Who's going to train it?"

"I will. I'm home all day, remember?" Vincent said. He gave me a look with those vivid blue eyes that I'd never been able to say no to, unless he was bound in ropes on the spanking bench. And even then...

When a person saw their doom coming from a mile away, and the control they thought they had over their life was put into doubt, it was a sobering reality-check.

I had no real opposition to the idea. Maybe having a four-legged animal around would be a benefit to us all. Was this the final straw in God's plan to domesticate me, when I'd thought I'd outsmarted them at every turn?

The woman who answered the door looked to be in her sixties, with dusky skin and an impressive amount of hair piled on the top of her head.

"Hello. Are you Nic?" she asked, gazing at Vincent.

I raised my hand. "I'm Nic. This is Vincent and this is Matteo. Sorry... They both wanted to come."

"That's okay. My name is Francine. The person I spoke to on the phone — Juno — said they were sending you to pick out a puppy for...someone else?"

"Yes," I said. "It's a bit complicated. But they want to surprise their partner with a puppy, and they trust us to find them a good one."

"Well, I only have two left from this litter. One girl and one boy."

Francine waved us inside and, once we'd removed our boots, brought us into a cozy living area where two pups made excited noises from a small, blanket-lined cage in the corner.

"Only two puppies left?" Vincent said.

"That's right."

"So if we take one, the other will be on its own?" Vincent said, glancing my way.

I rolled my eyes.

Francine smiled. "Hopefully it won't be too long before someone claims the last pup. Why don't you sit down, and I'll bring them both over?"

"Sure," I said.

We sat on the sofa as Francine scooped up a pup in each hand. She held one of them out to Vincent. "This little girl is black and silver."

She passed the puppy to Vincent. Watching Vincent gather the wee thing to his chest and coo to it in soft tones took any remaining will from me.

"That one's for Charles," I said, reaching out to pet the wiggling thing. "Juno wanted black and silver," I reminded Vincent.

"Well, that's decided," Francine said. "I'll put the little boy back in the pen."

"No, please," I hastened to say. "It has come to my attention that our household is in need of a good alarm barker"—I eyed Vincent and Matteo—"to keep the burglars away."

Vincent passed the female puppy to Matteo and held his hand out for the little male, while gazing at me with wide-eyed astonishment, until he took the pup from Francine and became enraptured. It yipped once in his face and proceeded to lick his nose, much to Vincent's delight.

"He's the more traditional salt and pepper color."

"Well, fuck me," I said, then remembered I was not at home. I blanched and made my apologies to Francine.

"That's okay, Nic. Bad language and dog ownership go hand-in-hand. It's not always a pretty business."

"Is that a warning?" Matteo asked, passing the female pup to me and getting a better look at the male.

Francine laughed. "Could be."

I took the tiny pup fated for Charles and held it against my chest. It gazed up at me with sweet brown eyes and removed the last of my resistance.

"I'd normally warn you against buying a puppy on impulse, but since he's the last of the litter, if you can pay for him, he's yours if you promise to give him a good home."

"Of course. We have a townhome with a fenced yard," I said. "Matteo and I work, but Vincent is at home during the day." Once I'd said it, I realized I'd outed us to Francine. I glanced at Matteo, but he shrugged and smiled.

Francine didn't ask for any further details. She must come into contact with all kinds of people and different living arrangements when she placed her puppies.

She glanced between us and smiled with kindness. "I'm glad someone will be home during the day. I don't believe in leaving pets on their own all week, but I know it's unavoidable sometimes."

"I assume you addressed all of this with Juno?"

"Yes. They said they're an artist, and their partner works from home. So they'll both be available to raise this puppy?"

"Yes."

"Well, I'll leave you to get acquainted for a minute and make sure of your decision. If you do decide to take the little boy, I'll need an immediate e-transfer for sixteen hundred dollars, since you won't be able to provide a certified check."

"Of course." I passed her the check that Juno had given me. "Here's the payment for the female."

"I'll be back in a moment with the papers. You'll have to sign, but there's also a spot for Juno. It can be faxed or emailed back to me so I can send in the registration."

She left the room to give us some space and allow us to make our decision.

Matteo had switched with Vincent and was holding the male puppy now, while Vincent held Charles' puppy. I held my hands out to Matteo with a resigned expression on my face.

"Give him to me, please."

Matteo handed him over. He was warm, soft, wriggly and fucking adorable.

I held his pudgy little body up in front of me so I could look him in the eyes while he scrambled for purchase.

"All right, now listen. If you come home with us, you will have to learn to pee and poop outside, behave yourself and not chew on inappropriate things or steal socks."

As I considered all the things that could go wrong, I caught glimpses of a chaotic future. But who could say no to that face? Perhaps I was a Big Bad Dom capable of reducing grown men to tears, but I knew when I was mastered.

"Here, take him," I said, passing him to Vincent, who gave the female pup to Matteo. "Come up with a name by the time we get home."

"Are you serious? We're going to buy a puppy?" Vincent said.

"Yes. I'm going to buy this puppy for you. Do you have a problem with that?" I went all gruff and businesslike when I felt vulnerable and terrified that a decision I'd made might come back to bite me in the ass.

"I don't, but I'm having a hard time believing it," Vincent said in hushed tones.

"How the hell am I supposed to say no when we're taking his only remaining sibling away?"

"You can say no. I've heard you."

Matteo laughed.

"What are we supposed to do, leave the poor thing here?"

They were both smiling when Francine came back in the room.

"So, have you decided?"

"Yes. We'll take the male," I said. "Matteo, can you send Francine an e-transfer from the expense account?"

"Yes, of course."

"That's wonderful!" Francine said. "My email address is on the form I gave you to fill out."

"Thank you," Matteo said.

Once the paperwork and payment were taken care of, Francine gave us some blankets to wrap the pups in for the journey, along with two large cloth bags.

"There's a food sample and a toy for each of them to get you started, and a list of instructions for puppy's first month. I'm sure this little boy will bring lots of excitement to your lives. Thank you so much for taking him, and please wish your friend the best with his pup.

Don't hesitate to get in touch if you need advice. Puppies are a lot of work."

Sometimes you have to just go along when things spin out of your control. It's the only way to keep your purchase. And occasionally, you get to places you never thought in a million years you'd go.

Vincent gave me the puppy to hold on the way home, and he and Matteo had chosen a name by the time we'd left the town of Stittsville behind. I cuddled little Musket in his cozy blanket while Matteo held Charles' as-yet-unnamed female pup. The sun sparkled off the powdery snow as we drove home with our tiny bundles of potential.

Let it be known that Nic Walker never shies away from an adventure.

At least it wasn't a human baby. We still had several months before Matteo's grandchild made its appearance. Perhaps I could practice my nurturing instincts on Musket so that by the time the baby arrived, I'd be able to handle that situation.

Taylor would flip out when he saw Musket. He'd never expect us to come home with a puppy, and I knew he'd be thrilled. Anticipating the joy he would experience made me happy. I was glad to have another person to help with the training.

It took about forty minutes to get to the apartment. We put the pups down on the snow for a pee before we brought them up. Francine had let us know that, at this age, the puppies would need to do their business every hour or so, and that any excitement or a meal or a big drink of water might speed that up.

I texted Juno to let them know we'd arrived. In a moment, they texted that Charles was busy with some cataloguing in the office, so it was perfect timing.

When they opened the door and saw two puppies, they were understandably confused.

"Hi! Wait a minute. Why are their two? We only need one!" they said, their voice hushed so that Charles wouldn't hear.

I held up my hand to stop them from panicking.

"This one's ours," I said, keeping my voice low, pointing to Musket, who was now in Vincent's arms. "That one's yours. It's a girl."

Matteo held the female puppy out to Juno.

"But…but you don't want a dog!"

"I never said that. And we couldn't just leave him there all alone." I glanced at the puppy in Vincent's arms. "And now I'm invested."

Juno laughed. "Wow. Who knew it would only take a little bundle of fur to conquer the heart of Nic the Great."

I flipped them the bird while they nuzzled the tiny female puppy.

"Oh my goodness! She's so cute!" They gathered the puppy to their chest and cooed at her. "Charles will be thrilled!"

"I should hope so for the amount of money we just spent," I said, pretending to be offended. "Anyway, Francine assured us she's black and silver, like you wanted."

"She's adorable. Charles is going to shit himself."

"Great. Not literally, I hope. Something tells me we'll be dealing with all the shit we can handle in a little while."

"Har-har," Juno said, approaching the closed bedroom door.

"Charles, would you come out here, please? Nic's here with Vincent and Matteo. They brought something for you."

"It's from Juno," I called out, "but we're delivering it."

We exchanged secret smiles and tried to keep the puppies quiet while we waited for Charles. The pups had fallen asleep in the car but now were awake and wriggly.

Vincent made faces at Musket, who kept licking him. Juno snuggled the female pup under their chin, which seemed to calm her.

"Wait a second. It's not going to pee on me, is it?" Juno said.

"No, they both had a pee on the front lawn before we came up," I said.

"Oh, thank God."

"You know you're going to have to take her out to pee every hour for the first couple of weeks, right?"

"Well, I'm hoping Charles will want to do all that."

I raised my eyebrows as the door to the bedroom opened and Charles walked out and into the living room.

He stopped dead when he saw what we were holding. His gaze went from one puppy to the other, then he gave Juno a questioning look.

"This one's yours, my darling. I hope you'll take good care of her."

Charles seemed spellbound by the sight of the tiny puppy in Juno's arms. Then he glanced at Vincent and Musket.

"Was there a sale? What's going on?"

Juno stepped forward and held the female pup out to Charles. "Well, funny story. They went to collect this little puppy for you, at my request, and they decided they couldn't bear to leave the last puppy with the breeder, all on its own." They gave me a haughty side-eye. "And Nic likes to upstage me."

"That's not—" I protested, but gave up. "Yes, and no, there was not a sale. These little beasties cost a fortune," I grumbled.

"Are you for real, Juno?" Charles said. "You bought me a puppy? It's really mine?"

"She's all yours, darling. You get to name her, and you get to take her out to pee and poo in the night. Isn't that wonderful?"

Charles laughed and gathered the tiny puppy to his chest, gazing at the three us with wonder. "I've always wanted a dog. My parents never let me have one. Thank you!" He pulled Juno into a close embrace that only ended when the puppy wiggled and started yipping because she was being squashed.

"I've got everything we need," Juno said, kissing Charles then nuzzling the puppy. "I stashed it all in the bedroom closet."

I put my hand on Vincent's shoulder. "I suppose we'd better get to a pet store and purchase what we'll need for Musket."

Charles looked over at me. "You really bought that puppy because you didn't want to leave it there?"

"Yep," I said, popping the 'p'. "I find it difficult to deny Vincent something he wants desperately, and he wanted this little guy. Maybe I'm softer than I let on."

Juno laughed sharply. "If that's not the truest statement in the history of statements."

"Shut up, you. It's all your fault."

"Clearly."

"All right. Let's leave Charles and Juno alone to welcome their new family member," I said, turning us toward the door.

We stopped at a Super Pet, and I volunteered to stay in the car with Musket while Matteo and Vincent did the shopping. They came out with two huge plastic bags and a plush dog bed that looked like it would suit a golden retriever.

"I knew this would happen. Does he really need a bed that big?"

"He *is* going to grow, you know," Vincent informed me as he kissed the pup in my arms while Matteo stowed their purchases in the trunk.

"What have we done?" I muttered, secretly thrilled but needing to play the part of put-upon father so badly that it hurt. "I know I'm going to regret this."

"I don't even care," Vincent said, starting the engine as Matteo got in the back. "Regret it all you want. Musket belongs to us, now, and there isn't anything you can do about it."

I grinned. I turned to the pup in my arms. "And now your Daddy's asking for a spanking!"

"Only once we've got Musket sorted out. I have to set up his bed and his food and water, then take him for a walk and—"

"I see how it's going to be. I'll be last on the list now."

"I'll have lots of time for spankings…and other stuff. Don't forget Taylor. He can help."

I felt a rising panic. "Now listen, both of you. We have Musket now, and Zarah's going to deliver her baby in the fall. I don't want any more additions to this family. I can barely handle you all *now*."

Vincent and Matteo smiled benignly as we drove home, and I quietly tried not to freak out, and to accept an unpredictable future filled with promise.

* * * *

It took Taylor zero-point-two seconds to fall in love with Musket. The look on his face when Vincent placed the puppy in his arms was priceless.

"Is he for me?"

"He's for all of us. Well, he's Vincent's pup. But we all have to help out."

"Oh my God, he's adorable! I have to call Riley! This is amazing!"

He clutched the puppy to his chest while he phoned his boyfriend and Vincent hovered nearby.

"Taylor, I need to take him outside," Vincent said.

"I'll only be a minute. Hold on. Riley? You are never going to guess what I'm holding right now... No, it's not a new dildo. Very funny... It's a puppy! Nic bought Vincent a puppy and he's—oh shit, he's pissing. He's pissing on me right now. Vincent! Fuck!"

Taylor gazed down at the yellow stain spreading across his T-shirt, then up at Vincent helplessly, then narrowed his eyes as none of us reached out to take the pup from him.

"You wanted to hold him," I said.

Taylor continued to speak into the phone. "Yeah. They're all just standing here watching, not helping me at all."

Riley's laughter could be heard, as Taylor grinned and shrugged, cuddling Musket closer.

Epilogue

Seven months later

Winter finally ended, spring arrived and summer after that. We got to know Zarah and spent time as a family together. Musket grew into a sensible, well-trained dog.

Daphne and Alexander got married, and the world went on as normal. Whenever I felt overwhelmed or uninspired during out sexual encounters, I had Vincent or Matteo take over Dom duties. Soon I'd feel my fingers itching to grab the reins again, and that would be that.

September, with its shorter days and cooler nights, breezed in to a general sense of anticipation. The call came during the third week of the month.

Vincent and I were enjoying some private time in the bedroom when Matteo knocked and apologized for disturbing us.

"What is it?" I said, when I'd opened the bedroom door.

Matteo stood there in his apron, holding a wooden spoon in one hand. He glanced past me at Vincent, who lay sprawled out, naked except for a pink camisole and lace panties, on the bed.

"Zarah's in labor."

Vincent jumped up and raced over. "Oh my God. This is it?"

"I think so," Matteo said. "Her friend called me from the hospital. The doctors say it's a go."

"We'll drive you. Vincent, get dressed. Matteo, turn off supper or get Taylor to take care of that."

"He's walking the dog. I don't think he took his phone," Matteo said, his expression suffused with anxiety.

"Oh. Well, turn everything off and leave a note."

"Okay. Yes. Good idea."

"Matteo, breathe. We've got lots of time."

How did I know that? Because I'd been reading up on all things labor and pregnancy-related. Now that I'd been presented with the miracle of childbirth in someone else's body, I couldn't find out enough about the process.

Zarah's husband, Dennis, had effectively vanished. Matteo had gone to the house with Zarah — with the strict promise not to engage in any physical altercation unless he was defending himself or her — to negotiate getting a few more of her belongings back, only to find the small bungalow unlocked and abandoned. Most of the items belonging to Zarah were gone, but she'd been able to salvage a few things.

Taylor had been sympathetic, since he knew what it was like to be in a controlling and abusive relationship, even if it didn't involve physical harm, and to find the miscellanies of your life disposed of without your consent. It had only been through tenacious intervention and fortuitous circumstance that we'd been able to get his things back.

Zarah had begun a new life, for herself and the coming baby. She was getting some counselling, which was helping a great deal. She was determined to make a life for herself and her child.

* * * *

We arrived at the Civic location of the Ottawa Hospital within the hour. Once we made our way to Labor and Delivery on the fourth floor, Matteo spoke with the nurse at reception while we found seats in the waiting area. He returned to us after a few moments.

"She's in Room 402. They're administering an epidural right now, so I can't go in. But I'll be able to join her in a few minutes."

"That's good. She won't be in pain, then."

"Hopefully. God, this is terrifying," Matteo muttered.

"What was Zarah's birth like?"

"All I remember is that her mother swore a blue streak during the entire process. It happened so fast."

The nurse called to Matteo from her place at the desk. "Mr. Rossi? You can go in now, but the others will have to wait here."

I grabbed his arm before he could leave and squeezed it. "Good luck. We'll be waiting for any news."

"Thank you," he said, and followed the nurse down the hall.

Vincent and I tried to be patient, but when we were well into the third hour, I wondered if it would be better to head home and come back when Matteo messaged us that the baby had arrived.

I stood up to go to the nurse at the desk, when the double doors opened and Matteo burst through them, his eyes brimming with excitement and a broad grin etched on his handsome face.

"The baby is here, and she's healthy and strong and gorgeous!" he announced as Vincent joined us.

"Congratulations, Grandpa!" I said.

Matteo blanched. "*That* is going to take some getting used to."

"A girl?" Vincent said, his voice pitched high with excitement. "I can't wait to buy her all the frilly little dresses she could want!" Then he glanced at me, apologetically. "Well, uh, unless you don't think —"

"I think that as long as we give her some other options, you can buy her all the pink and pretty clothes you'd like, Vincent."

Matteo laughed and said, "This little one is going to be spoiled. You can count on that."

"How is Zarah?" I asked.

"She's just fine. I mean, she's exhausted and it wasn't a cake walk, but she's so happy. Do you want to see them?"

"Of course we do! Come on, Vincent," I said, grabbing his hand and pulling him after Matteo, my heart filled with excitement and the promise of a brand-new adventure.

Northern Horizons: Repentance and Absolution
AE Lister

Coming November 2022

Excerpt

Oscar was gone, and I couldn't find him.

The brush surrounding the new homestead — if that's what you could even call it — grew dense and completely impenetrable in some spots. A fella could easily get lost, especially a city fella who couldn't tell an oak from a birch and fell o'er his own outsized feet on occasion. There were wolves in these parts that could kill a man Oscar's size in an instant — not to mention the bears, coyotes and panthers.

I'd told him time and again not to go wandering around without me, to stay near the ramshackle rooms we were fixing up and not to go looking for whatever he thought he wanted to see.

The kid was trouble. Had been since I'd first laid eyes on him, back in Dawson City, and there wasn't any way of taming him, much as I'd tried. I supposed, when it came down to it, I didn't want to tame him any more than I'd wanted to smother the fire that kept us both warm at night and reared up inside me when he looked at me the way he did. He'd nigh burned me with a primal passion that I was still trying to control — or at least understand. It still didn't make no sense how the two of us came together like we did. But there was no turning back now.

"Oscar!" I shouted into the trees, trying to see my way and take heed of any movement ahead of me. I'd searched all around the sorry excuse for a house that he'd inherited from his dead uncle, and he was nowhere to be found. So now, I headed into the brush toward the creek. I'd already checked the well and he wasn't there, neither fallen into it nor trying to get water up for a drink. I didn't know where he was, and I was beginning to panic.

"Oscar! D'you hear me? Get back here right now or I'm gonna tan your pretty hide so bad you won't be going anywhere for a week!"

As I stepped past a big boulder, something caught my eye. T'was the peacock-blue frayed edge of a shawl, and I stopped in my tracks when I saw a familiar person standing there, looking off into the distance.

"Cal? Is that you?" I said.

But it couldn't be Cal. Cal was back in Telegraph Creek, whispering scandalous things into the ears of men who paid for her time and attention. The person wearing the shawl turned with a languorous ease and smiled at me. T'was Cal sure enough, even though it couldn't possibly be.

"Jimmy! My, I'd almost forgotten how handsome you were."

I blushed, taking off my hat and giving her a puzzled look. "What're you doing here? How did you get here?"

Cal simply smiled, the dimple in her cheek on the opposite side to Oscar's. "Has that naughty boy wandered off again?"

She'd rouged and painted her face till there was no sign of the handsome boy underneath, the boy who was a girl for all intents and purposes, except for the tackle between her legs.

"Yes, he has," I said. "And I'm gonna haul him o'er my knee when I find him."

Cal laughed and pursed her lips. "Oh, I don't think he minds that, do you?"

"He'll mind it this time," I promised. "And he'll mind me."

No matter what games we liked to play involving my hand on his behind, giving him a pretend walloping for being a brat, I'd give it to him this time — like I had once before when he'd wandered off and scared me half to death.

"You know which way he went?" I asked Cal, since I had nothing else to go by.

"There," Cal said, pointing through the brush. "I heard a gunshot by the river."

My blood went cold. *Fuck.* God only knew what he'd wandered into, and for a goddamn second, I almost fell to my knees.

In a moment I'd moved past Cal and I was running, tearing through the brush toward the river, terrified of what I'd find. The crack of a rifle pierced the silence, and it echoed for long minutes as my breaths ripped through my chest.

When I found him, if he hadn't been shot or eaten by wolves, I was gonna kill him.

Just as I reached the edge of the brush, where it opened up onto the river, another shot echoed through the trees and I opened my eyes, gasping huge gulps of air and blinking at the darkness.

"Hey, hey, shhhh, it's okay. It's a nightmare. You're dreamin'."

Oscar's shadow loomed above me in the darkness of the room that was barely a room — just a space with four walls and a fireplace, the fire banked now but the coals glowing red.

I grabbed him and pulled him down to me, hugging him so fierce that he squirmed and protested.

"Stop. You're hurtin' me. I can't breathe."

I loosened my hold a little so he wouldn't try to get away, but t'was hard not to keep him in a death grip after that god-awful dream.

"What the hell's wrong with you?" he said, clutching my shoulders.

"I couldn't find you," I whispered, my heart beating a drum in my chest. "I couldn't find you." I was breathless, even though I'd not left my bed.

"I was right here — right here in this bed beside you, all night long."

I nodded against him, keeping him close to prove to myself he was here and he was all right — and so was I. His hair smelled of wood smoke and sweat, and I reckoned we could both use a wash.

"You need a bath," I murmured, kissing him under his ear where it smelled of his own special musk that I loved.

He snorted. "So do you. I reckon we oughta change into fresh underwear, too, and wash these ones."

I slid a hand under the blankets, popping the buttons of the flap of his union suit so's I could skate my palm o'er the swell of his ass, making him squirm in a delicious way, his small, stiff cock pressing against me.

"Well, dammit, it sure is you, Oscar. No one else has a nubby so small and sweet what wants to pretend to be big enough to cause any mischief," I said, teasing him the way he liked to be teased, so that he felt dainty and delicate and half the man I was. It had seemed strange at first and like he should be offended by that kind of talk. But he loved it, and that was a fact. And I didn't question it at all no more.

Sure enough, he groaned and pressed his fingertips into my shoulders, rutting against me like a dog.

"Goddammit. What were you dreamin' about? You were sayin' my name then you said *Cal*. Was it *scandalous*?"

"No. T'was terrifyin'. You were lost, and I couldn't find you."

He pressed against me, his nubby rubbing against my thigh through the fabric of his union suit. We'd bought the sets of red flannel underwear when the weather turned right cold at the start of November. Guess we'd had enough of freezing our asses off on our journey and we wanted to be warm, even if it meant looking ridiculous. "Well, you did, didn't you? You found me good, since I was right here all along."

"That's a fact. Thank the Lord," I murmured, turning his face to mine and finding his lips in the darkness. He opened to me in that sweet way he had of assuring me there weren't nothing I couldn't do that he wouldn't want, as far as any intimacy with his body went. We'd nigh explored every damned inch of each other by now, and I never could get enough of him. I wasn't sure I ever would.

I pulled away from his mouth and nuzzled into his neck, just to sniff that scent of him I was so fond of. "I'm just so relieved you're here and t'was all a dream."

He relaxed into me and offered his long neck for my kisses and for me to run my nose along. The bit of stubble there did something to ignite me, and I lapped my tongue o'er his Adam's apple, then bit it gently.

"Oh. Jimmy. Hell," Oscar breathed. "It ain't even dawn yet, and you wanna keep me awake?" He yawned.

"I'm sorry. Never mind. Just cuddle under these here covers with me. I need to know I got you."

Oscar stifled another broad yawn. "You got me, all right, in every sense of that word. You prob'ly won't want me after a few more months. I'm already a nuisance most of the time, ain't I?"

I didn't know if he was playing up being a brat or if he truly thought he was a nuisance.

"No, you're just— My ma used to call it restlessness, when I couldn't sit still. Said I'd grow out of it, and I guess I did."

"Yeah? What if I never grow out of it, huh? What if I'll always be like this?" Oscar said, snuggling into me, wiggling his ass, even though he'd just told me he wanted to sleep.

"Keep still. I'm tryin' to go back to sleep, and you ain't helpin'."

"What if I'm always this restless?" he asked again in a whisper. "Will you still love me?"

I laughed. He was all that and more, this twenty-one-year-old man-child.

"I reckon I will. Can't seem to help it," I grumbled, as if me loving Oscar was an inconvenience rather than the miracle of a lifetime that had been wasted with broken men.

"Good," he said, laying his head down on the feather pillow. "I reckon I'll still love you, too."

* * * *

In the morning, we woke to bright sunshine streaming in the new glass windows. We needed curtains. Next trip into town we had a list of things to buy. The big wad of cash I'd looted from Spook and Whitlaw — the outlaws who had stolen and almost raped and killed Oscar — still had some bulk to it. I reckoned that the money was rightfully ours, what with all the heartbreak and fear they'd put us through. Although, in the end, it had shown me plain as day how I felt about him — that I'd go through hell and back just to keep this man safe and by my side. I'd shot both of them outlaws dead without a thought, even though I'd sworn off killing when I'd left the gang. Figured I was doing the world a favor in that case.

Oscar and I — with help from Carson Moore, Timothy Jensen and Timothy's son, Frank — had managed to shore up one small room of the broken-down homestead that Oscar had inherited from his late uncle. T'was a decent-sized space with a fireplace and a cookstove to keep us warm and fed, but with the big bed on the other wall and a chair and a table in it, the room felt small and close.

That suited the two of us, though, for now, and made it cozy and easy to heat, although we were eager for spring to come so's we could finish the job and get at least a couple of more rooms added on to this one. T'was a huge job, for sure, but we had a will and the means, and I reckoned we could get some kind of decent home built for the two of us in time.

For now, I was content to wake up under the wool blankets and quilts we'd bought, snuggled beside Oscar, who sighed softly and blinked like an angel, even though the thoughts in his pretty head were more devilish, surely.

"Mornin', Jimmy."

"Oscar. How'd you sleep?"

He rolled onto his side and watched me. "Well, 'cept for you makin' so much noise and hollerin' my name, pretty well I guess."

I'd forgotten about my nightmare. Now it came back to me with all its ball-shriveling fear and sense of loss. I frowned.

"Don't remind me. I never want to have it again."

"I'm sorry. Maybe you won't."

I shrugged. The truth was, I'd been having a lot of bad dreams. Most of them were flashbacks to long-gone days, when I'd watched Whitlaw and Spook do some horrible, bloodthirsty things. And I'd done some myself. Seemed all that was coming back to me in my dreams, and I couldn't hardly get rid of it. I woke from those nightmares feeling hopeless and riddled with guilt, full of disgust at the way I'd lived my life. But this last one, when I was out of my wits trying to find Oscar, brought back all the terror of losing him to Spook and Whitlaw near the beginning of our journey and how lost I'd felt when I didn't know where he was or how I would find him before they killed him—or did something worse.

I gazed at Oscar, wondering how I'd ever deserved this handsome, heartbreaking lamb of a man and feeling like any moment God was gonna take him away from me. I didn't deserve Oscar. I felt that deep down in my bones, and I guess t'was coming out in my dreams. But for whatever reason, he loved me, he wanted me and he'd stayed with me all this time. Now we were setting up a home together, the way we'd do if Oscar was a lady and I wanted to marry her, make her happy and protect her.

I truly didn't see a difference. The fact that he had a cock instead of a cunt seemed entirely inconsequential. I'd bedded whores more masculine than Oscar. He had the sensitivities, delicacy of feeling and ability to nurture that a woman might. He'd taken care of his horse, Sprite, and he'd nursed the kitten we'd got when we'd first arrived in Port Essington. He'd coddled her like she was his baby, and now she was a big mouser with a fierce disposition that still had the tendency to curl up in his lap for loving when she needed it.

Of course, we couldn't let on in town what we were to each other, and that was a shame. But t'was a price I'd pay to keep Oscar close. I reckoned I didn't have to tell anyone what they didn't need to know. What me and Oscar did in our home was a private thing, and t'was gonna stay that way.

Oscar yawned and gazed back at me out of his sweet brown eyes.

"You look like you're havin' your deep thoughts again, Jimmy."

He kneeled up and took my face in his hands.

"You know it don't do to brood about stuff. You just wind up workin' yourself into a mess of feelings you ain't got no control o'er."

I nodded and sighed, because he was right.

"I guess t'was different when we were on the road. I was too busy getting us safely from one place t'other, I didn't have time to dwell on things from my past — or worry beyond our survival."

"The past is the past," Oscar said. "I told you that once, and I'll tell you that again. You ain't the same man. You told me a bit of what happened back then, and it truly is horrible. But you was misled and mistreated, and you ain't responsible for the things those men made you do. You gotta believe me."

I nodded in order to placate him, but I did feel responsible. The truth was, I could have left the gang earlier than I had. I could have distanced myself from those men when I'd realized what they were capable of — and I hadn't. I'd run with them for years, helping them with their thieving and killing and all-around terrorizing, because I was too lily-livered to leave. True enough that I'd hung in the background, but that wasn't an excuse.

But Oscar was right. There were things to be done and we'd better get at them, rather than brood under the blankets on this chilly, late-November morning.

"Let's get them horses fed and watered," I said, as a lump under the blankets at my feet started moving and making muffled mewls.

Oscar reached a hand underneath and pulled Sprite out into the day. The gray and white cat with enormous ears, named for the horse we'd lost to wolves just outside of town, blinked and stretched on the top of the blankets. She let Oscar pet her for two seconds, then jumped onto the floor to search for mice.

"I swear, those ears get bigger every day," I said. "She part rabbit?"

Oscar laughed. "Maybe. Anyhow, I think they're cute."

He hopped out of the bed and grabbed the poker from where it leaned against the iron stove, opening the hatch and stirring the embers that had mostly faded.

"We'd best get this stove goin'," he said, "before it gets too cold in here."

"Sure," I said, grabbing my pants and pulling them on. "Don't forget to do up your access hatch," I said, reaching out to cup his bare bottom in my hand.

"Fuck. That's your fault," he said, reaching behind him to button up the fabric flap.

I grinned. "It mostly always is. Pretty convenient to have that bit of cloth be moveable, I'd say."

Oscar laughed and gave me the wide, impish grin that I loved.

"That's a fact."

He winked as I pulled on my trousers and shirt, then sat to do up my boots, while Oscar threw a couple of logs in the stove and stoked it so that they caught and crackled.

We'd spent close to a week chopping wood that now stood in a huge pile against the outside wall of our makeshift house, helping to keep the cold out and in a convenient spot to grab when we needed it. Oscar had learned real quick how to use an axe, and his muscles had bulked up, although he'd always be on the lean side.

He was strong and he was healthy, and that was all that mattered.

Back when I'd found him—an aimless, wisp of a stray in Dawson City—he'd been skin and bones, and filled with a desperation so raw that it hurt to look at. I'd fed him and taken him back to my room to get him cleaned up so's he'd have half a chance. But what had happened the next morning I don't think either of us had expected.

Oscar had been full of gratitude for the kindness I'd shown him, and I'd been horny for something I couldn't hardly imagine until he'd put his lips around me and got me off that first morning, to my shock and his satisfaction. Those were the only skills he thought he had at the time, and I guess he'd wanted to show them off and thank me for what I'd done.

I'd been blindsided by his bold actions and the confusing feelings he'd aroused in me, but I should have known there wasn't any going back from that moment—that he'd claimed me then and there, and t'wasn't no use to fight it. As if something had possessed me in that room, I'd hauled his naked ass o'er my lap and spanked him like he was a misbehaving child, when he was the farthest thing from that. But we'd both got off and my world had tipped upside down and backward.

And now we were here, in Port Essington, building a home and making a life together. Back when I'd left the gang and taken up a good, honest career hauling supplies, I never would have expected anything near to this, and now I couldn't rightly imagine anything else.

About the Author

AE Lister/Elizabeth Lister is a Canadian non-binary author with a vivid imagination and a head full of unique and interesting characters. They have published 10 books, one of which received an Honorable Mention from the National Leather Association – International for excellence in SM/Leather/Fetish writing.

"Sensual and visceral BDSM." – Amazon.ca

AE Lister loves to hear from readers. You can find their contact information, website details and author profile page at https://www.pride-publishing.com

P U B L I S H I N G

Sign up for our newsletter and find out about all our romance book releases, eBook sales and promotions, sneak peeks and FREE romance books!